WATERY GRAVE

"Why doesn't he turn back?" Angelina asked. "Why can he be pursuing us? We have no cargo for him to capture! Is the man quite mad?"

"Yes," Ki said. "Didn't you notice that before? Yes, LaCroix is quite mad."

"We've bested him," Spinola said. "He can't swallow that. No pirate could. His crew would elect a new captain. We've bested him and the only way he can save himself from disgrace is to sink us. To sink us and see that every one of us dies."

And, Jessie thought, pirates had ways of dealing out exquisite death...

◆·◆ **WESLEY ELLIS** ◆·◆

LONE STAR

AND THE
GULF PIRATES

A JOVE BOOK

LONE STAR AND THE GULF PIRATES

A Jove Book/published by arrangement with
the author

PRINTING HISTORY
Jove edition/September 1986

ISBN: 0-515-08676-2

Jove Books are published by The Berkley Publishing Group,
200 Madison Avenue, New York, N.Y. 10016. The words
"A JOVE BOOK" and the "J" with sunburst are trademarks
belonging to Jove Publications, Inc.

PRINTED IN THE UNITED STATES OF AMERICA

★
Chapter 1

The paddlewheeler *President Grant* chugged and frothed its way northward, hugging the coastline. The blue waters of the Gulf of California were smooth as glass before the steamboat; behind it the wake frothed and fanned into a gradually vanishing V.

The steamboat had taken on its cargo at San Felipe, where the schooner *La Mesa* out of San Diego had off-loaded its cargo of lumber, hardware, and food supplies. The cargo was bound for Fort Yuma, a military outpost virtually isolated by the Apache, Heart.

The Colorado was running high just now. Within weeks, possibly days, the flood stage would be ended and not even a shallow draft boat like the *President Grant* would be able to negotiate the red river upstream to Yuma.

"There's a vessel coming up fast on the port side, Captain Easley," the helmsman said.

The bulky man in the faded-blue uniform and battered hat turned from his chart table and squinted from the wheelhouse of the steamboat.

"A fisher?" he asked himself. But he already knew it was no fishing vessel. It was a frigate in full sail, knifing through the water, canvas popping. It was a dark ship, an older one, but quicker than anything Easley had seen in the gulf before. There was virtually no shipping in these waters. The communities along the dun-colored coast were small, poor, not the sort of towns that brought in commodities by sea.

1

"She's going to cut across our bow if she maintains that tack," the helmsman said. He glanced back worriedly at the captain, who stared in puzzlement at the dark vessel.

"Give us twenty degrees to starboard," Easley said, and the helmsman complied. Gradually the ungainly paddle-wheeler changed its course enough to let the faster frigate pass safely.

"She's put her wheel over too, Captain," the helmsman said, and the captain of the *President Grant* nodded with irritation. The damn fool was going to come right across their bow. The frigate was much nearer now, larger. Easley couldn't see a hand on deck. The dark frigate was like a ghost ship, unmanned, malicious.

Something stirred uneasily in the back of Easley's mind. He walked to the communications tube, blew into it, and waited impatiently for his mate to answer belowdecks.

"Cassidy? Open the armory, arm all hands."

"Sir?" a sleepy, perplexed voice answered through the tube.

"Damn it, do as I say, do it now!"

But it was already too late. Easley saw the puff of smoke first and then the dark, rapid form of the cannon-ball. The report of the cannon finally reached his ears as the ball cut within ten feet of the steamboat's bow and splashed into the water.

Easley spoke quietly into the tube. "Forget it, Cassidy. Helmsman, full stop! We're about to be boarded."

Fort Yuma sat sweltering in the Arizona heat. The sun beamed down hard and white against the low, jumbled army installation. In the commander's office three junior officers watched as their CO wiped the sweat from his red face, poured a drink of whiskey without offering any, wiped the sweat from his face again, and leaned back in his squeaking leather-covered chair to glower at his officers as if they were responsible for the Apache war, the damnable sun, and the winds of hell that raced across the desert flats every evening at sunset to cover everything with grit, sting the eyes, and clog the nostrils.

"It's three days overdue," Captain Thaddeus York said. His stubby fingers drummed on his scarred desk top. Beyond his office window an NCO could be heard shouting commands to a group of unhappy soldiers drilling beneath the fierce sun. "We've lost another shipment, it seems. Damn all!" he exploded suddenly, thumping his desk with his fist. "Damn Heart, damn these pirates, whoever they are, damn Alfredo Guiterrez!"

The last-named man was the governor of the Mexican state of Sonora. York thought the Mexican government ought to be able to put a stop to the piracy, just how he never articulated.

"I need ideas, gentlemen. You know how things stand here. If I could get away with it, by God, I'd detach a company of cavalry and send it south."

Two of the younger officers glanced at each other, wondering just what cavalry was supposed to be able to do against a seagoing enemy.

"Ideas!" Captain York repeated loudly, reaching again for his whiskey bottle.

"I know someone who might be able to help," one of York's lieutenants said quietly. York's head snapped up and he stared at the junior officer.

Gleason was his name, Ford Gleason, and he was a first lieutenant in the U.S. Army. He was tall, slightly over six foot one, with copper-colored hair, deep-blue eyes, a straight nose, and generous mouth. He was well set up physically and he knew his business when it came to fighting. He took commands well, issued them intelligently, and carried himself like a gentleman. York found that he resented Ford Gleason for most of these attributes.

York himself was overage for his grade, balding, a gradually increasing fold of fat oozing over his beltline. He drank too much, had just been deserted by an unhappy wife, and he held no hope of ever being promoted again—

3

unless he could get those goddamned supplies upriver somehow.

"What," he asked with a tinge of sarcasm, "are you suggesting, Lieutenant Gleason? Hiring some outsiders to do army work?"

"If we can't do it ourselves, and we can't—we can't go south of the line, not without getting our entire officer corps lined up against a wall. Civilians, sir, it will have to be civilians if we hope to stop those gulf pirates."

"Civilians," York repeated, wagging his head heavily. He didn't like the very word. If he'd known then who Ford Gleason had in mind for the job he would have liked it a lot less.

No one else had any suggestion at all and Captain Thaddeus York could close his eyes and see those major's oak leaves flying away.

The businessmen of Yuma were up in arms. The army couldn't protect them or guarantee their safety. York looked dismally at his lieutenant and gave a quick nod of his head as if agreeing to some small crime.

Outside it was hotter than sin, the glare off the Colorado and surrounding white sand overwhelming. Lieutenant Ford Gleason used the post telegraph to send a wire. The lines had been up for nearly three days this time, a recent record. Heart knew well enough that the telegraph wires were an enemy of his. The blue soldiers could contact other blue soldiers hundreds of miles away and by means of those communications defeat him. Heart's solution was simple—defeat the wires themselves.

"Excuse me, sir," the red-faced corporal at the key said, "is this an authorized wire? It's not a military address." He examined the yellow pad where Gleason had scribbled his message.

"It's authorized. Route it through with your highest priority."

"Yes, sir," the corporal said dubiously. "If you say so."

The enlisted man looked again at the destination flag on the telegraph pad. Starbuck Ranch, Texas. And just what in hell business could the lieutenant have contacting that far-away place?

Gleason's eyes were on the young corporal and so the man turned to his key and began tapping out his Morse. He had just finished his message and received acknowledgment from his relay at Fort Bowie when the wires went dead again.

Ansel Barnes wore a white suit and flat white hat with a wide brim. He was in his fifties, rotund, gray-faced, and grim.

Barnes was taking charge of things personally this time. He was the Fort Yuma sutler among other things, responsible for supplying the soldiers at the post with writing paper, sweets, Indian-crafted goods, beer, and under-the-table whiskey. He also ran a hardware store for civilian Yuma. Neither of these enterprises was doing well at present. Damned army couldn't do a simple escort job. When the military brass had decided on shipping material from West Coast ports, chiefly San Diego, around the Baja Peninsula to the isolated and besieged town of Yuma, Barnes had been one of the first to applaud the move. There was no way that damned red scoundrel, Heart, could stop a ship from sailing up the Colorado River.

Then these goddamned pirates had appeared. Opportunistic bastards—the world was full of them, Barnes decided miserably. Out to keep him from making a decent living.

This time would be different. This time he was ready.

Barnes had traveled to the Mexican port of San Felipe, waited while his consignment of goods was transferred from the schooner *White Horse* to the Mexican-registered steamer *Mas Mal,* and sailed northward toward the mouth of the Colorado with his goods. And his personal army.

"Let the bastards try it," Ansel Barnes muttered. He stood at the rail of the *Mas Mal* as she steamed past the small dun-colored islands in the gulf toward the river. The sidewheeler was heavy with goods: planks and nails and

5

pig iron, trade trinkets, tinned food, and whiskey. The four eight-inch cannon she carried added to the weight.

From the wheelhouse the boat's captain called out, "Vessel on the port side, Mr. Barnes. Closing fast."

Barnes had a pair of binoculars around his neck. Army issue, bartered for a case of beer from a very thirsty and slightly disreputable sergeant at Fort Yuma. The sutler lifted the glasses to his eyes, focused them, and found the dark ship closing from astern. Barnes smiled grimly, feeling a sudden rush of excitement edged with fear creep up his spine to the base of his skull. He turned to the thick-chested man at his right and spoke.

"All right, Oscar, this could be it."

"I'll make preparations," Oscar said in his bearlike growl, and Barnes knew that Oscar McCann would do just that, and do it competently. McCann had been a sailing man, had been in the tough ports of Singapore and Shanghai, had fought in the Crimean War as a Turkish artillery officer and spent the last decade in the American West as a soldier, lawman, or outlaw depending on the opportunity.

McCann strode down the deck, calling loudly to his hired warriors. The canvas was whipped from the cannon and they were charged as McCann issued Winchester repeaters, handguns, and sabers.

Barnes repeated his smile. The bastards wouldn't get this shipment.

The frigate was closing still. Dark and ominous, all it needed was the skull and crossbones on the foremast. Barnes scanned the ship carefully, unable to see a single hand.

He did see the gunports open abruptly, silently, and he swallowed hard. There were eight ports on this side and through them now the flared black-iron muzzles of naval cannon appeared. Barnes looked to the wheelhouse and signaled the captain. There was no sense in trying to outrun the seagoing vessel and at Barnes's signal the sidewheeler's power was cut, the boilers sighing to a halt.

"Let 'em come," Barnes said, but the uneasiness he had

felt was growing to cold fear. "They won't want to blow us out of the water," he told himself, trying to bolster his flagging confidence. "Ruin the goods ... they'll try to board and then we'll have 'em."

But Barnes was no Commodore Perry, no Shanghai pirate, and the nerve was beginning to drain out of him. He looked with some trepidation to Oscar McCann, who was cool, bull-like, solid, arms crossed over his massive chest, which was encased in a red-and-white-striped shirt, and he felt a little better.

A starboard cannon on board the dark frigate suddenly belched flame and smoke and a ball crossed the bow of the *Mas Mal*. Barnes backed away and stood trembling with anger and fear, watching as the frigate dropped sail and swung toward them.

"Ready," he heard McCann say softly to his band of warriors—thugs, Indians, Mexicans, back-alley toughs. Barnes started to yell something, to order McCann to surrender, but it was too late already. "Take her below the waterline," the former sailor said, and three eight-inch cannon opened up in unison from the deck of the *Mas Mal*, the fourth misfiring with a backflash and a futile cloud of white smoke.

Barnes shifted his eyes to the dark frigate, seeing the cannonballs send up spumes of water, hearing the muffled thud of iron against oak planking.

Barnes was looking that way, slight hope rising, when the gunports of the frigate exploded with flame and smoke and sound and half a dozen cannonballs arced through the air to strike the *Mas Mal* solidly.

Planking flew into the air, splintered and broken, forming deadly wooden splinters as the boat rocked under the impact of the frigate's cannonballs. Barnes was hurled to the deck as flame jutted from the wheelhouse and Oscar McCann, hollering furiously, tried to organize his inexperienced gunners.

Two of the *Mas Mal*'s cannon spoke again, a deep-throated threatening sound, but the threat was hollow as the balls sailed through the rigging of the frigate without any damage but a torn shroud line.

The frigate, meanwhile, masterfully captained, had come nearly parallel with the *Mas Mal*, its gunports open, cannon primed. It hovered twenty yards off the port side of the steamer and then drifted nearer yet as Oscar's men rushed for their firearms.

"Surrender, surrender!" the captain of the *Mas Mal* was shouting from the wheelhouse, but no one seemed to hear him above the clamor of shot, of men screaming, timbers breaking, shouts, and panicked commands.

The gunners on the *Mas Mal*'s decks had retreated in blind panic, leaving their unloaded cannon, noses down, harmless. The frigate swung to and now with sharp panic Barnes did see her crew. Men appeared from behind the rails and in the rigging. Grappling hooks swung overhead and whined through the air to bite into the wood of the *Mas Mal*'s rails.

"Stand ready to repel boarders!" Oscar McCann said, and a bullet from aboard the frigate ripped his throat out. The big man staggered backward and then toppled into the clear blue waters of the Gulf of California, a strangled command or curse or prayer bubbling up.

Barnes's crew was in full flight now. Some went over the side and swam toward the miles-distant shore. Others made for the lifeboats as the crew of the frigate swarmed aboard the motionless steamboat.

Barnes drew a little-used derringer from his vest pocket and backed away, hand on the rail. Fifty feet from him a raider swung a saber with violent skill and lopped the head from a McCann thug. The body fell flopping to the deck, neck pumping crimson arterial blood.

Rifles fired close by Barnes as a few of his men tried to battle back. A flash of heat washed over Barnes and he heard the dreadful thud of lead against flesh as a charge of grapeshot ripped through the bodies of his defenders.

From the deck of the frigate a tall dark man wearing a red bandanna over his head gestured and a single round was fired from a brass swivel cannon. This one carried an incendiary load of some sort and as it impacted against the wheelhouse the upper deck of the *Mas Mal* burst into flame.

That was the last thing Ansel Barnes saw. A white-hot pain erupted inside his skull and blood flooded his eyes. He was blown back over the rail of the steamer as dozens of gun-bearing pirates charged down the decks of the *Mas Mal*, war cries or curses rising from their throats.

Barnes hit the water so hard that it knocked the wind from him. At this time of year the gulf waters should have been warm, but they seemed very cold. Icy fingers reached out and grasped him, tugging him down, and in minutes the fighting seemed very faraway and unimportant. The sky was a white, swirling thing and the distant shore a brown blur. Somewhere far distant a boat was burning on the water, but it seemed meaningless. There was some reason Ansel Barnes was trying to stay alive, trying desperately to swim, but at that moment he couldn't recall what it was, and he let the darkness of the water tug him down into the mermaid depths.

★
Chapter 2

Her name was Jessica Starbuck and behind those sea-green eyes was a knowledge of many battles. She stood waiting for the stage driver and the shotgun rider with the adoring eyes to throw down her luggage.

It was hot, dry. People walked numbed with the sun through the streets of Yuma, Arizona as if nothing could stun them from their heat-induced lethargy. But men's heads lifted and women's eyes narrowed at the sight of the honey-blonde woman with the perfect figure, full, firm breasts and heart-tightening little buttocks.

She wore a green skirt and jacket, white blouse, black boots, and Spanish-style flat-crowned black hat. Her face was tanned, green eyes bright, blonde hair loose and sun-streaked. The shotgun rider nearly fell from the stage roof as he tried to toss a trunk and simultaneously squint into the sun at the apparition below him, that soft-voiced, loin-stimulating woman who represented everything Cab Hollister had ever dreamed of and never before seen.

The man with her was tall, deferential, lean. His eyes were dark, the way he held his body indicative of physical competence. He showed no apparent jealousy of the beautiful woman, but he was watchful all the same, and Cab Hollister for some reason was careful not to meet the tall man's gaze, although the shotgun rider had seen his share of fighting both in the War and on the desert, where white raiders and Apaches made his continued existence precarious.

10

The man, the one the woman called Ki, might have been Indian himself. He was dark, but not as dark as an Indian. His hair was straight, cut off carelessly at the shoulders.

He might have been Chinese, like the Go-Luk clan that had helped build the railroad and now ran their little shops down along the river, keeping to themselves, but this Ki wasn't that either. He was too tall, his face too narrow. Whatever he was, he was a man—and God, was that a woman!

Cab Hollister managed to step back from the stagecoach without permanently crippling himself and absently accepted two silver dollars as a tip from the soft hand of his goddess.

"How far is it to the fort?" Jessica Starbuck asked.

"'Bout a mile, miss," the shotgun rider answered. His hand, silver coins gleaming in it, was held open before him. His eyes lay adoringly on her face. If she had asked, Cab Hollister would gladly have piggybacked her up to Fort Yuma. She didn't ask.

"Ki? Shall we walk?"

"It is a hot day," Ki answered. "Why don't we wait a while and see if Ford shows up? I wired him from Fort Bowie."

"Lines are down between here and Bowie," Cab Hollister advised them. "Heart again."

"The Apache?"

"That's right. Bastard'll hang one day—beggin' your pardon, ma'am—and I'll be there applaudin' . . . if I live that long," he amended. Heart had nearly gotten his scalp twice. Cab didn't believe in the third time being a charm. "I'll find a kid and send him up to the fort if you like," he offered. "Cantina over there's got a ladies' dining parlor, good food, and cold beer."

He nodded toward a plastered-adobe structure three doors down from the stage depot.

"If you would, I'd appreciate it," Jessie said. Cab's

11

hand was still thrust out and she dropped another silver dollar into it, but the shotgun driver never noticed it.

"Manuel's kid—call him Paco—he's always hangin' around the stable. I'll send him. He's always glad of the chance to ride."

"Fine. Have him ask for Lieutenant Ford Gleason, please. Tell him Jessie is here."

"Jessie. Yes, miss, I'll do that. Lieutenant Gleason—I know him. Good man."

"I think so," Jessie agreed. The shotgun rider's eyes narrowed.

"You know him, do you?"

Jessie acknowledged, "We've met."

They had more than met. They had been allies once and then friends and then lovers. It looked as if they were to be allies once again. What remained of the other facets of their relationship she didn't know.

Cab Hollister watched as the two strode off toward the restaurant, scratching his head. He didn't get that pair. They weren't the common sort you ran across and knew right off what they were. A drummer looked like a drummer, a cowhand like a cowhand, a schoolteacher like a teacher. These two didn't look like anything Cab could put his finger on.

But, Lord! Wasn't she a fine-looking woman. He pulled his hat down a little and went off yelling for Paco.

Cab Hollister could have scratched his head all day and still never figured out Jessie and Ki. She was more than a beautiful woman, he more than a tall man with dark skin. Jessie's father had been one of the wealthiest and most influential men in the country, owner of a worldwide trading empire. Alex Starbuck's death had left his empire in Jessie's hands and she had managed it well.

Again, she was more than just a canny businesswoman. She was a woman weary of lawlessness, with the fortitude and ability to combat it when regular law-enforcement agencies were incapable or unwilling. She had seen some bad men and a lot of trouble, but she had survived. In her

12

valise was a .38-caliber pistol that Alex Starbuck had had mounted on a heavier .44 frame. The double-action Colt was slate-gray in color with polished peachwood grips. It was a lovely thing to look at, but like Jessie herself it was more than a showpiece. The gun had seen some use and would see more.

Cab Hollister would have been surprised to learn all that and surprised to learn that at the moment he had been talking to the lady with the green eyes a little derringer had been riding on her thigh beneath her skirt.

Maybe, pondering it all, Cab would have understood all of that about the lady. Ki would have confounded him completely.

The man was half-Japanese, half-American, and he was a master of *te,* the art of empty-hand fighting. Concealed in Ki's leather vest were numerous pockets containing throwing stars, *shuriken.* With a speed the fastest gunfighter in the territory would have had trouble matching Ki could with seeming effortlessness pick a fly off the ear of one of the stagecoach's horses.

The *shuriken* had deadlier uses as well.

Whether Cab knew or understood any of this, Lieutenant Ford Gleason did. That was the reason he had sent for these two. Gleason's face was bright with pleasure when he found Jessie and Ki in the restaurant, both sipping tea, Jessie nibbling at toast.

"Jessica."

She half rose, hesitating slightly. It had been a very long time, but Ford's arms went around her waist and drew her to him and she felt an electric charge rush through her body, felt her thighs press against his in an unconscious gesture of desire. The feeling was so strong and sudden that it nearly overwhelmed her.

"You look fine, Ford," was all she said as she withdrew to look into those deep-blue eyes, to examine the coppery hair, the wide slash of a mouth, the wide chest and narrow hips of the army officer. "Just fine."

"You're a dream," Ford said. His tone was intended to

13

be light, but there was a quiver of emotion in it. "Ki." He stuck out his hand and had it wrapped up in the callused, powerful fingers of the *te* master.

"Glad to see you again, Ford," Ki said.

The soldier reversed a chair and sat down, arms on the back. It took him another minute before he could detach his gaze from Jessie.

"Do you want to talk about it now?" the blonde asked. "Or someplace else?"

"Here's as good a place as any," Ford said, waving away the waitress. "There's no secret about any of it. If you talk to anyone in Yuma they'll tell you the whole story."

"Highwaymen, was it?" Ki asked. The telegram hadn't carried much detail.

"Pirates," Ford Gleason said, flashing an Irish smile that faded immediately to a look of concern. "Believe it or not."

"It's hard to believe," Ki said. The only sea they had seen was the seemingly limitless sea of sand around Yuma.

Jessie took a bite of her toast, a small bite that revealed her white teeth and pink tongue. Ford found it oddly provocative. Provocative enough to cause a small stirring in his loins.

"Yes," he said quickly. "This is what's been happening. We've got an Apache named Heart out here and several roving bandit gangs—Mexican-based. They know all of the freight routes and damn me if they don't seem to know or guess all the schedules. Getting supplies to the fort and the town of Yuma overland has gotten damned near impossible."

"Surely the army can protect its own supply trains," Jessie commented.

"Think so?" Gleason grinned wryly. "We *should* be able to, but it hasn't worked. Coming through Jacumba Pass last month, for instance, the freighters found the trail blocked—the only trail down that rocky hellhole. There

14

was an escort of fourteen soldiers. How many Apaches were in the rocks we could only guess afterward. Enough," Ford said, "to make sure there were no white survivors."

"Sounds brutal."

"It was. It is. There's no way to avoid those passes, no way to defend yourself once you're caught in them. Overland freight from California has come to a virtual standstill."

"And the pirates?" Ki asked.

"I'll get to it, Ki. I want you to understand the whole picture. When we pursue Heart it's nearly an exercise in futility—you know the Apaches. They disappear into the sand or the rocky hills or slip across the border. Heart's clever enough to know what that border stands for."

"We have a treaty with Mexico," Jessie put in.

"The pursuit treaty? Yes. When the Mexican *federales* or the U.S. Army is in close pursuit of a band of renegades they have the theoretical right to cross the border, but the Sonoran governor, a man named Guiterrez, doesn't like it at all. Afraid of Yankee invaders, I suppose. He fought in the Mexican-American war and he's stored away some bitterness. You're from Texas, you understand what I mean from the other point of view."

"There's a lot of Texans who will never forget that war," Jessie agreed.

"The main point is," Ford went on, leaning back, stretching his arms, "we're never in what you could call close pursuit anyway. Heart is a murderous bastard, but he's a good general. By the time we've chased him that far south he's gone with the wind—and the bandit gangs in some other part of the territory are raising hell, knowing that the army forces are split. It doesn't do much for our reputation. The local newspapers rake us over the coals, but the simple fact is we're spread too thin to do what they demand. It's driving my commander crazy."

"Thaddeus York."

"Yes," Ford answered. "He's not a bad officer, really,

15

but this is crippling his career and he's gotten to where he makes some bad decisions. He'd do most anything to clip off Heart's ears."

"The pirates," Ki prodded again and Ford smiled, holding up a hand.

"All right, this is where the pirates come in. Someone at regimental level came up with the seemingly shrewd idea of bringing supplies from San Diego and Los Angeles via the Gulf of California, upriver by paddleboat and safely to the fort and the town of Yuma. The Colorado's running high right now and those steamers don't draw much water. On paper it seemed like a fine idea."

"On paper," Jessie echoed.

"Yes. What has been happening in fact is that someone, I have no idea who, nor does anyone else, has been pirating the goods and army supplies before they reach the mouth of the Colorado. Once the goods are transferred to a slow-moving paddleboat in San Felipe—that's on the east coast of the Baja Peninsula, hundred miles or so down— the pirates have a field day. No way a steamer is going to outrun a big sailing vessel, no way she's going to get into an exchange of cannonballs . . . though Barnes tried it," Ford mused.

"Barnes? Remember," Ki said, "we just arrived in Yuma."

"Ansel Barnes is a local businessman. Our sutler, as a matter of fact. He was determined to bring his stores through and he hired a private gang of thugs, bought four cannon somewhere and tried to shoot it out with the pirates. He was blown out of the water. He lived, but he was one of the few who did. You'd think Blackbeard had raided his boat, the *Mas Mal*. Men hacked up with sabers, some tortured, an Indian woman raped, then murdered."

"The Mexican authorities haven't been able to do anything?" Ki wanted to know.

"No. They've made gestures, but Guiterrez isn't too concerned with American army supplies being taken in the gulf. Besides," York added with a shrug, "the Mexican

16

navy isn't exactly world-class. They haven't got a single gunboat in the Gulf of California and any they could bring in would be little more than a rowboat with a cannon astern."

Ford Gleason looked from Ki to Jessie and back again. "Maybe I've brought you two out for nothing. When I stop and think about it, I'm not sure what you could possibly do. We're all pretty much in the same boat. Piracy is a little unusual in the Southwest, to say the least. Can't lead a cavalry charge or ambush the bastards."

"Every ship docks," Ki said quietly.

"In a Mexican port. And the army isn't going to be allowed down there."

"We'll need a ship," Jessie said quietly, assertively. Ford Gleason just stared at her.

"And where," he laughed, "would you get a ship?"

Ki had to remind Ford, "You must remember that Jessie's father began his career as a merchant in San Francisco. Import and export to the Orient built the Starbuck empire. I assure you, Jessie has access to many ships."

"But that would take some time . . . to get a ship to the gulf."

"It will take some time," Jessie agreed. "Are your telegraph lines up?"

"Temporarily, yes," Ford answered.

"Then I have a wire I want to send. Antonio Spinola in San Diego," she said, looking at Ki.

"A Mexican?"

"Portuguese. A man who has sailed many seas and knows what we need. A hard crew, a fast ship."

Ford just looked at the woman with wonder. He knew the Starbuck empire had many resources; still it amazed him that Jessie could simply send a wire and have a gunship sent to the gulf.

"This Guiterrez," Ki said, "we must have his cooperation. An American gunboat in Mexican waters could bring many dark ramifications."

"Ki's right," Ford said. "We don't need an international

17

incident. The problem is, Guiterrez is obstinate, anti-Yankee, and totally uncooperative."

"Perhaps," Ki said, "we can change that."

"If we can do that, you two are magicians."

"There is always a way," Ki asserted.

"Then you've never locked horns with Alfredo Guiterrez. For now," Ford said, rising, his chair's legs scraping the floor, "we've got another miracle to perform. Smaller, perhaps, but equally important."

"Yes?" Ki's eyebrows lifted.

"There's no way that wire is going to go out to your friend in San Diego unless the captain approves it. The battle is going to be in convincing him that you're capable of doing what I've asked you to do."

Ford Gleason didn't feel that confident himself. Two people. A ship five hundred sea miles away. A recalcitrant Mexican governor. And a stone-eyed, skeptical commanding officer. Looking into Ki's dark eyes and the green, determined eyes of Jessica Starbuck lent Ford some confidence, but not much. If they believed they could do it, though, he was eager and willing to help them try. Maybe the old man could be convinced as well.

After all, what other choice did the army have?

Captain Thaddeus P. York couldn't do anything but sit and stare from behind his desk, his face flushing to various hues of red and purple as his twitching hand inched nearer the drawer where his concealed whiskey bottle lay.

He wasn't sure what he had expected. A gang of Texas bandits, former Rangers, a band of Comanche Indians—anything but what he now saw before him.

A Chink and a skirt.

"What are they supposed to be able to do about this situation, Ford?" the captain asked for the third time. "Just *what?*"

Ford Gleason had tried to explain this twice. This time he just replied. "She has a ship, sir. It's worth a try."

18

Thaddeus York gave in to temptation—the civilians be damned—and reached for his whiskey bottle. He drank three fingers of liquor down before the flush in his face faded a little to a gray pallor and, shaking his head heavily, he answered.

"What the hell. It doesn't cost anything. I'm a ruined man anyway. You understand that, lady? I'm ruined anyway." He leaned forward on his elbows, trying to ascertain if Jessica Starbuck—Lord, what a woman, look at those young jutting breasts!—understood his predicament.

"Then, Captain York, it can't get much worse. Only better."

"Yes." There was logic to the woman's words, but Captain York wasn't bolstered by logic. He was a man of force, and damn all, he wanted force! Not a Chink and a skirt. He leveled a finger at Ford Gleason, nearly dropping the glass that rested in the same hand. "This is your caper, Gleason. Yours! I'm not officially involved. I *won't be* officially involved. You're on leave as of this moment. I'll have your leave request predated and filled out properly. You are detached—unofficially but mandatorily detached. You understand me?"

"Yes, sir."

"I mean," York said finishing his whiskey, "you are *detached*. I don't want to know what you three are up to. I don't want any reports coming to Fort Yuma—especially no *written* reports, understand me?"

"Yes, sir."

"As for the rest of it—it's foolish, no, it's *stupid*. But if you think something can be accomplished, get to it. I just don't want the United States Army involved in whatever it is you think you are doing. Understand me?"

"Yes, sir."

"Then get out of here. Get going before I change my mind," Thaddeus York said, and as the three of them, his lieutenant, the Chink, and the skirt filed through his office door, he added under his breath, "and good luck to you, because if you can't do something, Regiment is going to shave my ass to jerky."

Looking in the drawer, the captain discovered that his bottle of bonded bourbon was empty. He sighed and rose to search for the spare quart in his filing cabinet.

★
Chapter 3

Lieutenant Ford Gleason wore black jeans, a faded-blue shirt, and a fawn-colored Stetson hat, sweat-stained up to the band. In the end Captain York had gone even farther with his "detaching" of Lieutenant Ford Gleason. He had come up with the idea of having Gleason resign his commission, and that request was now locked up in the commander's office safe, to be broken out if necessary. Officially Gleason was now a civilian and if all hell broke loose in Mexico his former commanding officer couldn't be blamed.

Gleason turned at the sound of footsteps and beamed as Jessie emerged from the fort's guest cottage to stand in the brilliant sunlight. She wore a divided buckskin-colored skirt that molded itself nicely to her bottom and to the lines of her thighs. She lifted a hand and, smiling, came to Ford, kissing him on the cheek—a brushing quick kiss that nevertheless caused a glow of pleasure to flow through Ford Gleason's veins.

"Is that all right?" she asked. "The kiss, I mean."

"It'll do for now."

"I didn't know if officers on post were supposed to do that sort of thing."

"You'd be surprised what goes on on post," Gleason said. "Besides, I'm not exactly in the army anymore," and he told her about Thaddeus York's brainstorm.

"Nice to know he's standing behind you," Jessie said with a small frown.

21

"Way behind? I don't blame him. York is tough on failure, tough on himself and his men. If this does somehow work out right he'll be generous with rewards."

"Captain's bars for you?"

"Probably," Gleason answered.

"You're still all army, aren't you, Ford?" Jessie asked.

"Still am. Just like before."

"Yes," she said and looked away into the distance, beyond the fort's walls. She only looked back when soft footsteps announced Ki's arrival.

Ki looked fit and alert in jeans, collarless shirt, leather vest, and cotton slippers. He looked into Jessie's eyes, seeing something hidden there, but whatever it was filtered away even as he watched.

"Are we nearly ready?" Ki asked. They had sent their telegram to San Diego and received an acknowledgment, and had decided in the interim that it was necessary to speak to the Mexican governor, Guiterrez. If he could be convinced somehow that eliminating the pirates was to his benefit as well things could be done much more easily. And legally.

"We'll need a few supplies," Ford Gleason said. "It's a long hot ride over mostly empty land."

"The sutler's store?" Jessie asked, looking across the parade ground to Ansel Barnes's establishment. Ford shrugged.

"If you like."

"I want to talk to the man anyway."

"There's not much he could tell you."

"Maybe not. But he was there," Jessie said. "He saw them."

Ki had another question: "The next shipment, Ford, when is it due in the gulf?"

Gleason's eyes shuttled to Ki's. Quietly he said, "Four days. A ship out of Los Angeles should reach San Felipe then. This one is all army materiel . . . and it is absolutely secret."

"The others have been secret as well," Ki replied. "It didn't stop the pirates."

"There's no way to keep it secret once the ships are in the gulf," Ford said, spreading his hands. "The only safe port along that stretch of coast is San Felipe. The seagoing vessels have to put in there. Anyone sitting on the dock knows what's up when they see a ship put in to port, see a river steamer alongside it."

"Break the chain," Ki said.

"What?"

Jessie said, "Ki means that there must be some way to do things differently. Find another port, transfer the goods at night. Something."

"Maybe," Ford Gleason responded. "But if there is a way, no one's come up with it yet."

They had reached the sutler's store. Stepping onto the plank walk they brushed past three soldiers in alkali-stained uniforms. Their heads turned slowly, their eyes growing intent as Jessie passed. One of them inhaled deeply, his neck stretching out, and the others laughed.

Inside the store was nearly empty, a few soldiers browsing, two in the corner drinking bottled beer. Behind the counter a lean, part-Indian clerk stood lazily.

"Is Barnes in?" Gleason asked.

The Indian's eyes narrowed and grew blank. Slowly his head inclined toward a door to his right.

Ford Gleason led the way to the office. Tapping, he was answered by a grunt and the three of them entered to find a dark room redolent of leather and cedar. At a desk a shrunken man sat, arms draped across his lap.

There wasn't much left of Ansel Barnes just now. Part of his scalp had been badly burned. His hair grew in tufts from his damaged skull. His right arm was twisted abnormally at the elbow. There didn't seem to be any flesh on his bones. He was a far cry from the man Jessie had heard described, that resolute, pugnacious storekeeper determined to teach the pirates some manners.

"Ansel?"

"Who's that?" the croaking voice asked, and Jessie realized that Barnes was nearly blind. "Gleason? Out of uniform?"

"It's me." Ford Gleason perched on the corner of an apparently unused, dusty desk. "Two friends with me." He made the introductions to an unresponsive Ansel Barnes.

"What do you want?"

"Just talk. We're going after the pirates, Ansel."

The change in Barnes was deep and violent. The word triggered off a lot of hatred and frustration, fear and confusion. "Kill the bastards, kill them all," the sutler growled. His cheeks had turned crimson, his bony hands clenched into fists. His eyes, dull and lusterless, brightened, and stared into the distance. "The army's finally going to do something, are they?" He looked at his hands. *"Now."*

"Not the army, Barnes, not officially. Miss Starbuck, Ki, and myself. We're going to have a try at it."

Ansel Barnes was silent for a moment and then he roared with unexpected laughter, throwing back his head, shaking with the gales of amusement that washed over him. "Forget it!" he said with a savagery that soon puddled into limitless melancholy. "They'll kill you," he said sadly. "Cut your throats—take the young woman and use her. They can't be beat. Not by the likes of you, I know."

Jessie asked, "Will you tell us what happened? Exactly."

Barnes looked up at her, shook his head, and took a small, whistling breath of air into his lungs. "All right. Why, I don't know, but I'll tell you."

His voice was matter-of-fact, but his hands remained clenched and small pearls of perspiration popped out across his forehead. When he was through he was shaking with the memory of what he had been through.

"Is that it?" Jessie asked. "There's nothing else you recall?"

"I've told you all of it."

"The ship—can you describe it better?"

"Dark. Sixteen guns, I think."

"A frigate?"

"That's what I said! Four masts. Very fast."

"The crew—what nationality?" Ki asked. "Could you tell?"

Barnes thought a moment and shrugged. "Mixed. Some Indians, thought I saw a Chink. Couple looked Malaysian —sailed there once when I was younger. Mexicans. Few Americans or maybe English . . . don't know. Their captain was dark, tall. Younger man. Earrings, bandanna around his head."

And that was all Ansel Barnes could remember or cared to remember. There wasn't anything else to be learned there and so Jessie and the men thanked him and went out into the sunlight again. It was nearly a hundred degrees outside, although it wasn't yet noon. A dry wind whipped light dust through the air in shifting veils.

"I want to send another telegram," Jessie said.

"To Antonio Spinola?"

"No, to the International Ship Registry in San Francisco," she said.

"You heard something in there?" Ford nodded toward the sutler's store.

"Nothing in particular, but I began to wonder. How many gunboats can there be in these waters, Ford? How many frigates? A ship that size doesn't just appear from nowhere. It was built by someone, sold to someone for a certain purpose, maybe retired and refitted, but a four-master doesn't just appear from nowhere and begin a career of piracy."

"If we knew what ship it was, how would that help us?"

"I want to know *who,*" Jessie said. "Who is behind this and why."

"Simple profit is behind it," Ford Gleason said with a laugh.

"Is it? Maybe," Jessie said, "maybe."

Ki filled up several burlap sacks with supplies while Ford and Jessie sent the second telegram. He purchased four half-gallon canteens, the largest Barnes had in stock, tinned meat and salt biscuits, a camp knife, and a box of .38-caliber cartridges for Jessie's Colt.

It was easily done, quickly done. Ki had prepared as well as possible for the trek south across the desert. Just a small task, one that should have been completed without trouble.

No one told the drunken soldier that.

The man was hunched over a bottle of beer, eyes red and aggressive, sleeves rolled up over massive forearms. His uniform sleeves were empty of chevrons, but a darker patch of material showed where there had once been three stripes.

"Chinks," Ki heard the man mutter. The word was followed by a belch. Ki ignored him. This wasn't the time, the place. There were other things to be attended to— horses to be saddled, packs to be made up.

"Chinks," the man muttered again, "seen 'em on the UP. Eatin' raw fish, squatting down, talking their gook tongue. Ain't Christian, ain't human."

"Shut up, Dart," a second soldier said.

"Don't tell me what to do," the man named Dart snarled.

"Use your brains. You already lost your stripes. Want to go back in the brig? Man's a civilian . . ."

"I said *shut up!*" Dart shouted. His big hand shot out and gripped the front of the other soldier's shirt, tearing away three buttons.

"Thanks," the soldier said woodenly. "I'm going back to the barracks to change." He pried his shirt from Dart's fingers and stumped to the door. Dart glowered, lifting a whiskey bottle from under the table, taking a swallow before he returned to staring at Ki.

"How much?" Ki asked the Indian behind the counter. The breed was watching Dart with dark eyes that showed patience and a deeper, nearly hidden hatred.

"Ten dollars. Eighty-seven cents."

Ki counted out the money deliberately. He knew the

26

man behind him hadn't forgotten about him. He could feel the malevolence focused on his back.

The soldier had troubles. What kind Ki didn't care to know. But he had troubles and was drifting into that state of mind where a man simply doesn't give a damn. He obviously had no fear of the army authorities—they had already busted him, placed him in the brig. Liquor was oiling the skids for the soldier, and Ki was a convenient target for his every frustration and prejudice.

"Thank you," Ki said. He shouldered the burlap sacks and stepped toward the door.

Dart stepped in front of him, face flushed, eyes sullen and bloodshot. Ki sighed. Was there no end to these confrontations, to the numbers of men who had a few drinks and wanted to batter someone?

"Pardon me," Ki said, and he stepped sideways. Dart positioned his body in front of Ki again. This time when Ki sighed there was a curse mingled with the exhalation.

"Where you goin'?" Dart demanded.

"My friend," Ki told him, "where I am going is not your business. You don't want me here and, believe me, I am happy to leave. I have my life and my business to attend to. I mean to get on with it—I suggest you do the same."

"Very nice," Dart said belligerently. "Very good talkin' for a Chink. Good English, boy."

Ki stiffened only slightly. "Thank you." He started around Dart again and again had his path blocked by the big soldier. The man reeked of tobacco and sweat and alcohol, and some deeper, subtler scent like that of a rotten tooth—perhaps the scent of Dart's own decay.

"You'll leave when I tell you you can go," Dart said, and then he made a large mistake. His big hand shot out to grab Ki's shoulder, but Ki wasn't there. A reflex too quick for Dart's numbed mind to follow or appreciate had caused Ki to automatically jerk back, turn one shoulder slightly and pivot.

Before Dart could regain the balance he had lost Ki was behind him walking toward the door, bags shouldered.

27

Dart roared with all the frustration that was locked up inside him and he lunged at Ki, big fists bunching into burls.

He was going to kill the Chinaman, wring his neck, gouge his eyes out and maybe cut out his tongue like the Apaches had done to Private Fears.

Dart was going to do all of that and much more, but he didn't get the chance. The Chinaman turned and Dart had a glimpse of a hand, middle knuckle protruding, flashing through the space between them, tapping him lightly on the forehead. It seemed to be nothing but a tap, but Dart's knees buckled and his eyes unfocused.

Dart dropped to his knees, looked up vacantly at the tall man and then flopped forward face-first, his skull ringing off the planking of the sutler's floor.

Two corporals, one wearing an armband, burst through the door, and the Indian behind the counter simply pointed at Dart sprawled on the floor. Ki continued out the door, meeting the dry air, the wicked heat of the noonday Arizona sun with pleasure. It was clean and good and empty of disease.

Jessie and Ford Gleason were waiting at the paddock when Ki arrived. Gleason was saddling an army bay, one that had somehow escaped branding. Jessie was stroking the muzzle of a sleek, stubby gray with a splash of white on its flank.

She turned sea-green eyes to Ki and said, "All right?"

"Yes," Ki answered, "everything is all right. Where are the packhorses?"

Half an hour later the three of them trailed out of Yuma, following the Colorado, which flowed wide and deep between reddish bluffs. There were quail in the mesquite along the river and Ki watched as a sidewinder, pale and deadly, slithered away at their approach.

Ahead was Mexico, a long desert, bandit gangs, Heart the Apache renegade, and a dark frigate with a pirate crew. Ki wondered briefly what he was doing there, why a man would put himself in such a situation, but then he had made his promises—and looking at the honey-blonde who rode ahead of him on the gray horse, he knew why he continued on.

Japan had not been a home. A half-white was not respected there. He had left there as a warrior hunted, a price on his head. What home did he have, had he ever had except with this daughter of Alex Starbuck?

He had sworn to protect her, to teach her, to guide her. He had taken a warrior's oath and a man like Ki does not take such oaths lightly. He would protect her. He would do as she wished.

Just now she had made her decision, and when Jessie had decided, she followed through to the end. She would see the pirates defeated or die trying.

The sun seemed to be fixed overhead, a glaring white ball in a white sky. The sand was white, sculpted into graceful dunes, endless and eye-stunning.

Ki's thoughts continued to drift from point to point as his eyes shifted constantly, scanning the dunes, the bluffs above the river. He had been in hard country before and he knew that the empty land holds secrets, violent secrets.

Jessie and Ford were riding close together, their thoughts only on each other, and so it was Ki who saw the distant dark figures first.

The Apache were watching, trailing them southward. He looked again to Jessie and the army officer, but it didn't seem to be the time to interrupt them. There was no hurry at all. The Apache were distant still, and there is nothing more patient than a stalking Apache. There was time—until Heart's warriors came, and then perhaps there would be no time at all.

★
Chapter 4

Dusk was a dull, fading purple glow above the dunes, the river going slowly from blue to deep red and then to the same deep violet as the sky, the sand changing hues rapidly, forming blue shadows among red dunes that stood like a frozen sea.

The doves winged homeward from their watering places and quail began to call along the river's edge. A coyote challenged the coming night with a mournful howl and the Colorado flowed on.

Their camp was made early, the fire built and then extinguished as coming night crowded the sunset sky into flickering submission.

Ki sat apart, ears alert. He had still not told them of the Apaches following. It was time, however, it was time. "Heart?" Jessie asked when he informed them.

"Apaches. That is all I know."

"You saw them following us?" Ford Gleason was incredulous. "I saw nothing, and this is my country, my warground."

Ki refrained from saying that Gleason had seen nothing but Jessica Starbuck's eyes, her young, pert breasts, her throat and thighs all day long.

"They are out there. Perhaps they don't have enough men to attack, perhaps they are only waiting for dark," he said, looking to the sky, where only a thin filament of red-gold hovering over the far hills remained as a memory of the lost day. "Be wary—" Ki rose. "If you have no objection I shall stand first watch."

He withdrew then into the dunes and became a part of the coming night as the shadows settled around him and he crouched against the still-warm sand, waiting, listening, watching.

Ford Gleason watched Ki vanish into the night. Then he moved around the dead fire and sat beside Jessie in the sand. "It's all right?" he asked, and his eyes caught that last thread of sunset and gleamed softly.

"What's that, Ford?" Jessie asked.

"Everything . . ." The man reached for words. "I mean, he's still there, in the back of your mind, isn't he? Longarm, that is. When's the last time you saw the marshal?"

"Not long. In California a few months ago."

Ford Gleason nodded slowly. He was a long time in responding. "How was it—seeing him?"

Jessie inched nearer to him. Her hip met his and she took his hand. "It was good, Ford, it was very good seeing him."

"I thought so."

"But he's not here, Ford. I don't know when I'll see Marshal Long again. If ever. He's far away and you're here. Do you know what I'm telling you?"

His head turned slowly toward hers. "I hope I do," he said quietly.

She leaned toward him, head lifting, and her lips met his in a soft, openmouthed kiss. She took his hand and placed it on her breast and held it there. Ford Gleason understood then what she was telling him.

"A blanket," he said.

"Now?"

"Here—and now." The urgency was obvious. The need, the sharp uncontrollable desire for Jessica Starbuck. She nodded, rose, and picked up a blanket, tugging Ford Gleason to his feet.

31

They didn't go far. Fifty feet into the dunes. There, as the first stars began to blink on, blue and hard in the summer night, Jessie took the army officer down.

She slipped from her clothes in minutes and then her hands were at his belt, unbuckling it as Ford reached out, took her head by the back of her neck and pulled her mouth to his, searching it hungrily.

Jessica laughed and started to pull away but Ford pulled her to the earth, groping for her smooth, nude buttocks, dragging her to him.

Jessica met his kiss for a long moment then knelt over him, her hands roaming his body, across his chest and hard thighs, returning to the unbuckled belt at his waist, her head bending low to kiss his hard abdomen as her fingers tugged up his shirt and reached for the buttons on his trousers.

Ford lay back, his eyes filled with starlight and need. The woman kneeling over him hummed as she worked, undoing his trousers, her body swaying gently from side to side so that her marvelous pink-nippled breasts moved with gentle, erotic motion. Ford's hands cupped those breasts, their warmth filling his palms. His thumbs worked across her nipples, teasing them to prominent tautness.

Ford lifted his head and took a nipple into his mouth as his hands dropped between Jessica's thighs, working their way through the soft pale bush there to find her damp cleft.

Jessica tugged Gleason's trousers off and his erection sprang free. She laughed and he smiled at her, clinging to her as she straddled him, slipping him quickly inside, her warm body enveloping his, her mouth finding his eyes, ears, throat, and chest with demanding kisses.

Jessica straddled the army officer, her head thrown back, her hair cascading over smooth shoulders and breasts and she sighed with deep pleasure as Ford Gleason arched his back and drove it in deeper. She could feel his need, his strong pulsing wish for release and she encouraged him, her fingers finding the base of his shaft, teasing it as her

32

body worked against his with practiced skill, leaking its own warm fluids.

Ford half sat up, wrapped his arms around Jessie and kissed her hungrily, mouth, throat, breasts, his hands clenching her smooth, firm buttocks as she swayed and pitched against him, moving in primal rhythm.

Her mouth was open now, her eyes half-shut with ecstasy as Ford drove into her, against her with a steady, needful rhythm. She felt joy rising into her throat and she swallowed a muffled sigh of deep pleasure, her head swimming as she nearly fainted, collapsing forward to lie pressed against him, her breasts flattened against his muscular chest as Gleason continued his even stroking, a stroking that became an urgent series of thrusts, and Gleason gasped as well, his back arched, thighs trembling as a hot flooding completion filled Jessica with his seed.

It was that moment the Apaches chose to attack.

They rose up from out of the sand and charged, war cries echoing in their throats, toward the camp. They found the camp unexpectedly empty. Ki, watching from the dunes, had seen them coming, but his soft whistles of warning had gone unheeded. No matter—Jessie and Ford Gleason were above the camp in the dunes, lost in sexual delight.

The Apaches, silent and then suddenly jubilantly noisy, had burst into the camp, weapons raised, and had found themselves in an effective, unplanned crossfire.

Ki had his first *shuriken* in his hand, and as the Apache warrior silhouetted himself against the field of stars above the dune, the throwing star whipped from the *te* master's hand, singing through the air before it bit into flesh and cartilage, ripping the throat from Ki's target.

Jessie's thoughts had been far away, her emotions involved in the act of lovemaking, but the first Apache war cry had triggered an instant response. Rolling from Ford Gleason's body, she had dived for her .38 Colt revolver, and now, naked, on her knees, she triggered off three

33

shots, the barrel of the double-action revolver lifting with each muzzle flash.

Her first bullet was a wide miss. Impossibly wide until she saw the reason for it.

Her target had jerked aside at the moment she triggered off, jerked aside and then flopped crazily to the sand, a *shuriken* imbedded in his throat.

Jessie's second target was an Apache with a war lance charging the dune where she knelt beside Ford Gleason. Her .38 slug ripped through chest muscle and touched the heart of the Apache, and he was flung back to die against the sand, dark blood staining the dunes.

"Look out!" Ford Gleason shouted. Before Jessie could turn she saw the Winchester-armed Apache leap from a dune, his painted face savage and dark. Beside her Ford's own rifle spat flame and the Indian was blown from the dune to lie writhing against the ground.

It was still suddenly, the night empty, the stars bright. Jessie was aware of the chillness caressing her naked body, the scent of gunpowder, the deeper, feral scent of blood.

She rose cautiously, reaching for her clothes. Ford, naked himself, guarded her movements with his cocked rifle. Jessie paused, listened, heard nothing. The night belonged only to the wind now, to the wind and the distantly howling coyote.

"That all of them?" Ford asked.

There was no answer to that question. Jessie shook her head and dressed quickly.

The night held its breath while they both dressed. Ki was near the cold campfire when they returned, moving cautiously down the slope of the dune, their legs knee-deep in sand.

"Any more of them?" Jessie asked.

Ki shook his head. "There's no way of knowing. If there are more around, the shots will have caught their attention."

"You think we should move?"

"Yes," Ki said, looking to the dunes, blue and shadowed beneath the stars. "I think so."

They rode out quietly, the horses' hooves whispering in the sand. The river was lost behind the brushy bluffs to the west. There was no conversation. Each of them was lost in his own thoughts, bloody thoughts made more ominous by the darkness of night.

When the moon rose it glistened on the dunes coldly. Breath steamed from the horses' nostrils as the desert night turned bitter cold. Ki shifted constantly in his saddle, watching the trail behind them, marked clearly by their horses' hoofprints, but he saw nothing. Not then.

It meant nothing—you did not usually see an Apache until he wished you to. Ford Gleason had fought the Apaches before. Ki and Jessie had known a few as well. They preferred fighting afoot, unlike the Plains tribes with their mobile, efficient cavalry. It wasn't beyond the Apache to lie half-buried in the sand for hour after hour while the enemy approached, then suddenly to rise up and strike with deadly skill of arms.

If Heart was out there, if he wanted them badly enough, he would take them. Ki had the idea, perhaps mistaken, that their handful of goods, their horses wouldn't interest the Apache warlord that much, that they had had a chance encounter with a band of hunter-raiders.

There was always that hope.

Sunrise was brilliant, a golden band along the desert horizon that flared up briefly into deep orange and then became a pale-hued sun rising slowly, changing to yellow and then pure white as the sands, now flattening toward a long, empty playa, turned from blue to violet, to red and glaring white.

At dawn the desert was briefly alive with native animals. Rabbits fed or loped away; doves flew low across the land, veering away at the riders' approach. A coatimundi clung to a smoke tree, watching warily. Distantly Ki saw fleet, wary desert sheep spring away.

They rode on into the playa—a dead, limitless thing stretching southward, a dead sea where nothing lived. Cracked segments of ancient seabed like paving stones formed the floor of the playa. The horses plodded across it, shambling, heads down. It had been a long night.

"There's a water hole ahead," Ford Gleason said. "In those rocks." His finger pointed toward a jumble of chocolate-colored stone scattered across the desert floor. "We'd better water the horses while we can."

The sun was a burning brand across their shoulders and faces. Ford Gleason's hands were blistered with the heat. They found the water hole by winding up a narrow trail through the rocks.

And there they found the sign of many horses.

Ki swung down, let his horse drink, and stood frowning, head turning from side to side as he surveyed the dark, towering rocks around them. It was a bad place to be caught in, perfect for an ambush, and the riders of those horses hadn't been gone very long.

"Who were they, Ki? Apaches?" Jessie asked.

"I don't know who they were. Not Indians unless they are all riding stolen horses. All of them were shod."

"Boot tracks," Ford Gleason said. He removed his hat and wiped his forehead. "Bandits, it looks like."

He showed Ki and Jessie the tracks, plain and fresh in the mud beside the deep water hole. A crow sailed past, cawing angrily at this violation of his water rights.

Ki crouched down, touched a finger to the imprint of a boot, and looked again to the rocky hills. "*Bandidos*. You have many of them?"

"The area's overrun with them. A man named Rojas is the worst of them, the most powerful. They call him Águila—the Eagle. He raids south of the line and runs north, takes what he can in the States, and drifts south again. He's a murderous bastard; they say he's part-Apache himself. Self-styled revolutionary. It's easy enough for him to gather a peasant army around him. These dry-land farmers don't have much, a little dry corn in good years, maybe a chicken or two. He offers the young ones guns, bullets, horses, a cause."

"A cause?" Jessie said.

"Strike back at the rich landowners, take what should belong to them." Ford shrugged. "The usual stuff."

"Yesterday," Ki said, looking again at the tracks. "Perhaps last night. How many men, Ford? Thirty, forty?"

"It's a good estimate," the army officer said, studying the maze of horse tracks. "Too many for us."

"Water the horses," Jessie said. She looked around, shuddering. "Then let's get out of here. A bad place, isn't it Ki? Very bad."

It was a bad place. Water was scarce in the desert and anyone who needed it was likely to go to the few isolated springs where it could be found. That included Heart and this Rojas.

In an hour they were back on the trail, riding southward again beneath the burning sun.

"Guiterrez," Jessie asked Gleason, "how does he live out here?"

"Very well," Ford answered, laughing. The laugh hurt his lips, which were becoming blistered and split, and he touched a finger to them. "His casa is a massive place, three stories, set on a planted hillside overlooking the gulf."

"He must be a rich man."

"They say so. All Mexican governors are relatively wealthy, and a lot of them use their positions to grow more wealthy. Among them all, however, Guiterrez supposedly stands high. He has a stable of fine Spanish horses, a daughter whose every whim is satisfied—if it means importing lace from Portugal or silk from China—a wine cellar unmatched between San Francisco and Mexico City, and an army of *peones* to do his bidding."

"All of this money—legitimately earned?"

"Who knows?" Ford shrugged. "Apparently his is a land-grant family, very old. I've only seen him once when the authorities on both sides of the border were trying to

37

hammer out a more meaningful pursuit treaty as a way of hunting down Heart. Guiterrez is tall, silver-haired, obstinate—and he hates the *norteamericanos*."

"Heart raids on the Mexican side of the line too, doesn't he?"

"Yes, but Guiterrez would prefer to believe he can handle Heart himself. Heart and Águila."

"We need his help, Ford; isn't there some weakness in the man?" Jessie asked.

"Only for his daughter. Angelina is her name. I haven't seen her, but she's purported to be beautiful, haughty, demanding."

"Spoiled aristocracy."

"They say."

"Just the sort of man Águila Rojas is against."

"Or claims to be. Rojas doesn't strike me as any more than a border bandit—one with unusual success," the army lieutenant said. "What are you thinking of, Jessie?"

"Just turning it over in my mind," she answered. "There has to be some way to convince Guiterrez to help us stop this piracy. Some way."

"If there is, the army and a dozen American diplomats haven't discovered it yet. Rojas . . . how could he be helpful?"

"I don't know," Jessie replied honestly. "But there has to be a way to put leverage on the man. What's that?" she asked suddenly, pointing southward toward the mirrorlike mass gleaming beneath the hot sun.

"Just what you've been waiting to see, Jessie. The Gulf of California. The sea of pirates."

Nearer to the gulf the mirror brilliance of the water cooled to a deep blue. The sea was still and smooth. Only ripples of breakers touched the white sand beaches beneath the brown bluffs where thickets of nopal cactus flourished.

"How far to Guiterrez's house?" Ki asked as they sat on their horses on a seagrass-darkened dune above the inlet.

"Five miles." Ford's head lifted, indicating the eastern

shore. "If this doesn't work, Jessie—if we can't beg or convince the man to help us—what do we do? We're in Mexican territory and anything we attempt without official sanction is going to be as illegal as what the pirates are doing."

"We will do what we have to do," the honey-blonde said. She looked steadfastly at Ford and then winked, breaking into a smile.

"Even if it's illegal?"

"I didn't come this far," she said, "to worry about the technicalities. I came to crush these pirates. We will do it, Ford, one way or the other."

★
Chapter 5

The Casa Guiterrez was tall, vast, white with red Spanish
tile on the roof, surrounded by a white adobe wall and a
forest of nopal cactus. Nearer the house there was an acre
or so of lawn, great oak trees jutting skyward, huddling
protectively around the house.

There were uniformed guards at the iron gate and the
three riders held up as the two armed men stepped into the
road, rifles held diagonally across their chests.

"What is it?" they asked in English. "What do you want
here?"

"We would like an audience with the governor, Alfredo
Guiterrez," Jessie answered politely, flashing her best
smile at the guards. They didn't respond to the smile.

One of them, mustached, very dark, answered, "His
Excellency will not see you."

"Is Señor Guiterrez at home?" Ford Gleason asked, lifting his eyes to the big house.

"His Excellency can see no one," the guard answered
mechanically. He seemed to be gripping his rifle a little
more tightly. It seemed that "His Excellency" was going to
see no one except over his dead body.

"I had papers of introduction," Jessie said as she fished
in her pockets, "but unfortunately they seem to be lost."
She had no papers and searching through her pockets
wasn't going to produce any. What happened instead was
that two twenty-dollar gold pieces somehow found their

40

way from her pockets to her fingers, which they slipped through to lie gleaming in the dust.

The guards didn't miss it. They didn't miss a thing. One of them stepped forward and planted his polished boot on the coins. He nodded at the other guard and looked up at Jessie. "My friend will see if His Excellency is in."

It was a fifteen-minute wait before the second guard, perspiring now, returned. He nodded positively, but his eyes were not happy. "The governor has graciously consented to speak to you, Señorita," he reported. Jessie started her horse forward, leaving the two guards to stoop and recover the coins from the earth.

The trail wound once around the knoll rising from the bluff, through a colonnade of stunted cypress trees, and onto the flat ground above. From there they could see the jewel-like blue gulf stretching out for miles. The air was filled with bees and the scent of flowers.

Before the big house they swung down beneath the oaks and had their reins taken by a boy in *peon* dress. Jessie stood for a moment looking at the three-storied house with its arched windows and then she nodded.

"Let's give it a try."

Up five curved stone steps they walked to a massive, carved door of dark wood. A hollow-eyed, cadaverous man in a dark suit and red sash opened the door for them and stood aside.

The big man with the silver hair stood halfway down a staircase, one hand on the marble banister. He nodded to himself and then proceeded slowly down to greet his visitors.

Alfredo Guiterrez might have been called a curmudgeon, a petty dictator, or an out-and-out bastard, but he was also a man of the old school and one who appreciated beautiful women.

He walked to Jessie, smiling deeply, even white teeth showing. He bowed, took her hand, and kissed it. "Señorita, you brighten my house with your presence."

41

Jessie smiled in return, though there was something in the governor's eyes that she didn't like. She introduced her companions and Guiterrez nodded briefly to each as if Jessie had introduced her servants or given the names of her pair of trained hunting dogs.

"Please," Guiterrez said, gesturing broadly with his arm, "come into my study and tell me what it is you wish."

He took Jessie's elbow with his hand and steered her into a room off the vast vaulted foyer. The study was elaborately done in dark wood and green leather. Books in leather-and-gilt bindings stood in tall, glassed-in cases along three walls.

Guiterrez went behind his green-leather-topped desk and sat down. Taking a cigar, which he trimmed with a tiny pair of silver clippers, he lighted it.

"Now, then"— Guiterrez blew out a plume of smoke— "what is it that brings such a lovely young lady to my house?"

Jessie had been studying the huge portrait of a dark-eyed, feline Spanish woman in her twenties on the wall opposite. Angelina Guiterrez? If so she was extraordinarily beautiful, apparently haughty, and sensual.

"There are pirates operating in the gulf waters within your area of responsibility," Jessie said, jumping to the point. "We want your authorization to stop them."

"Pirates?" Guiterrez's brow furrowed deeply. He waved his cigar-clenching hand in a gesture of dismissal. "There are no pirates in the Gulf of California, young lady, you are mistaken."

"The hell she is," Ford Gleason said softly, but Guiterrez heard him and his dark eyes shifted to the young army officer, flickering slightly.

"Apparently," Jessie said, rushing on, "they operate out of San Felipe, or at least have contacts there."

"These pirates?" Guiterrez said as if patiently listening to a child's incredible tale.

"Yes. They have taken numerous boats carrying supplies to Fort Yuma and the town of Yuma."

"In Arizona?" Guiterrez asked, looking at his cigar.

"Yes, that's correct."

"I have heard nothing of this." He shrugged. "I have heard nothing of a Mexican craft being attacked in these waters."

"The victims have all been American ships," Gleason said.

"*Ah!* American! You see then, how would I know? What makes this business that might concern me? It is something the *Estados Unidos* must look into. No, this does not concern me."

"But it's taking place in your waters," Jessie said.

"I know nothing of it. No one has reported this to me," the governor protested.

"That is exactly what we are doing now," Ki said. It was the first time he had spoken and Guiterrez looked at him with an expression of surprise, as if he had forgotten the Japanese-American completely.

"Even if this is so," Guiterrez went on, refusing to admit that it might be, "I can do nothing. Mexico City is the proper place to lodge a complaint. This is an international problem, hardly one a local governor should be looking into."

"And if we notified Mexico City?"

"They would consider it and, of course," he said with a smile, "refer the matter to me."

"And you would ignore it," Ford Gleason said. The soldier was no diplomat. He irritated Guiterrez and it was obvious.

"I would do whatever I was instructed to do by my superiors," the governor said coldly. He rose abruptly, the interview apparently over. "Having received no instructions, I can do nothing. *Buenos días,* good day. Thank you, young woman, for brightening my own day."

Jessie looked sharply at Ford, who was growing red in the face, and the soldier tried to calm himself as he rose and walked slowly to the outer door.

"Your own daughter is exceptionally lovely," Jessie

43

said. "That was her portrait in your study, wasn't it?"

"Yes," the governor answered. "My daughter, Angelina. She would be happy to serve as your hostess, I am sure, but just now she is with her aunt in Alta California."

That, Ki thought, was one way of avoiding the offer of hospitality. This was a country known for opening its doors to travelers. It was nearly unthinkable for Guiterrez not to offer them drinks, food, beds.

At the front door Guiterrez again kissed Jessie's hand, bowed curtly to the two men, and left them to his doorkeeper who quietly ushered them out of the house to stand on the porch, the sea breeze gusting over them, shaking the big oaks.

"Well, we tried," Ki said.

"Bastard," Ford Gleason said. "Bastard politician."

"That doesn't do much good," Jessie said.

"No." Gleason rubbed his elbow. "Neither did coming here, though. He knows what's going on in Sonora and across the gulf in Baja. You can bet he's got ears and eyes everywhere. He just won't lift a finger to help the *norteamericanos*."

"He knows now that we are here," Ki observed, "and he didn't order us not to do anything. Just pointed out that there wasn't any authorization for it. Maybe it was his own way of being cooperative."

"Damned funny way," Ford complained. "Well?" He looked to Jessie. "What now?"

"Now," Jessie said, looking southward, "we go on to San Felipe. If the governor doesn't know what's going on, the people there sure do."

"They won't talk," Ford Gleason said. "They wouldn't dare."

"Maybe not. We'll see about that. All I know is when that ship arrives from Los Angeles the day after tomorrow I intend to be there, standing on the dock, watching for myself."

And that was that. If that was the way Jessie was going to have things, that was the way they were. They waited

44

for the *peon* to bring back their horses, well rubbed down now, mounted, and rode down the long trail from the big house. Glancing back once Ki saw the dark figure of a man at the upstairs window, standing, watching.

"You know, Jessie," Ki warned quietly when they had reached the gulfside trail that wound its sinuous way southward, "Ford may be wrong when he says that the people of San Felipe will not talk to us, but of this I am certain—it is very dangerous for us to be *asking* any questions."

"We will use caution, Ki," she said with cheerful optimism, and the matter was dropped, although Ki rode on gloomily for some time.

It was after dark before they reached San Felipe. They could see little in the darkness—the jutting shape of hills behind the town, the cubes and squares of the buildings themselves, a long wooden pier running out into the dark water, farther on the masts of fishing boats, some with lanterns hanging from their booms or glowing in portholes.

The town smelled like a mingling of fifty worlds—tamales and fresh bread were being made somewhere, beef sizzled, the smell of fish was pervasive and nearly rank. The bay itself was rich with scent. It lay quietly, its dark placid surface concealing many secrets.

"There are no large ships in port," Ki observed.

"No, there wouldn't be. The pirates have their own port somewhere along the coast. Maybe on the islands," she guessed, nodding toward the bay where small forms like irregularly shaped breasts floated on the water.

"How many islands are there, Ford?"

"Hundreds. Not too many where you'd expect to find anchorage for a frigate, I wouldn't think. That's something we could ask about."

"Cautiously," Ki said, using Jessie's word. She laughed, but not loudly. There were many men along the docks where they now rode, talking in low voices, some mending nets by the light of storm lanterns, others sharing a bottle of tequila, hunched down, faces hidden in a shadow—

45

watching. Watching the strangers who had ridden into San Felipe. Ki had the idea it wouldn't be long before the pirates knew that they were there—not that they posed a threat to them just yet, but something very odd had happened in San Felipe; three North Americans had ridden in without apparent purpose. And they asked too many questions, too many.

"We should have a story," Jessie said as if she had been inside Ki's mind. "Cattle buyers?"

"We could say that, yes." Ki smiled. "Is it any safer if they believe we are carrying enough money to buy a herd of cattle down here? A knife across the throat—then they discover we are not so rich."

Ford thought much the same way. "If anyone asks, we're waiting for the *California*, the ship out of Los Angeles. They'll think we're just three more stupid Yuma merchants with ideas of how to protect our goods."

"Why not," Ki said, shrugging. The odds were that no story would be believed anyway. They made a strange trio.

"There," Jessie said, pointing at a building with "Hotel," a word common to both languages, painted shakily across its face.

"It doesn't look like much," Ford Gleason said.

"If they've got a bed, it's enough for tonight. The saddle's worn me down and the heat's knocked me for a loop. If there are little critters in the beds, let them enjoy themselves. They can walk all over me tonight without waking me up."

"It might not be too bad an idea," Ki said, "to let the critters keep you awake just a little."

"You saw something?" she asked.

"Three men. They turned into an alley when I glanced back. Now, they are behind us again."

"Coincidence? How could they know already?"

"Coincidence, perhaps," Ki answered. "But I am not ready to place much confidence in coincidence just now, are you, Jessie?"

"No. Not just now," she agreed. She swung down as if

46

there were nothing at all on her mind, as if Ki hadn't spotted the men in the shadows. Loosening their cinches, taking their saddlebags but leaving the provision sacks, they walked into the hotel to be met by a wall of sultry air that the ocean breeze hadn't had time to push away yet.

Behind the counter a heavy woman in a striped dress sat eating frijoles and tortillas. She stood, wiping her fingers across her greasy apron, patting at her hair, which was knotted at the back of her skull, decorated with a black Spanish comb.

"Si, bien venido, welcome."

"We would like beds and a meal if you serve food."

"Food, yes. Three beds, yes," the woman answered, her smile hasty, uncertain, her eyes drifting to her plate where her own meal sat cooling.

The meal was plain, hot and filling, the beds, despite Jessie's earlier prediction, clean and apparently critter-free. Her room was between Ford's and Ki's at the end of a narrow upstairs hallway. Only Ki's room had a window and he stood in the darkness for a long while, breathing in the bay air, letting his eyes search the alley below, listening to the small rustling sounds Jessie made before she settled into her bed with an audible sigh, and the creak of the bed's leather strapping.

"You are down there," Ki said softly to the night. "Why, I don't know. Who you are, I don't know, but I can *feel* you out there."

There wasn't any sense in staying up the entire night watching and waiting for something that might not happen, and Ki was as tired as Jessie. He stripped off his shirt, kicked off his rope-soled slippers, and stretched out on the bed, arms behind his neck, flexing his shoulder muscles a few times, locking his hands together, squeezing and then pulling, loosening the unused tendons and joints.

He fell off to sleep almost immediately and drifted into a strange dream. Chinese junks pursued him across a sea of desert, rolling rapidly along on their wooden wheels, although Ki kept sinking into the sand. . . .

47

His eyes popped open and he came instantly alert. *Something.* He listened, eyebrows drawing together. How much time had passed? How long had he been asleep?

The sound came again and Ki recognized it for what it was, the squeak of a floorboard in the hall. It could have been a guest or the owner of the hotel, but Ki was suddenly wary. The steps were too stealthy, too quiet.

On callused bare feet Ki crossed the room, his own steps as silent as summer rain. He paused at the door, placed his ear to the wood, and listened. Then he smiled grimly. They *were* out there, and it was Jessie's door they were approaching.

They never got there.

The *te* master swung his door open and glided into the hallway. The two men there reacted instantly. One of them chose to run, boots pounding down the hallway. He was short, squat, and much smarter than the man he left behind.

This one—tall, scarred, dressed in a shabby vest and torn sombrero—turned, his face wolfish and hungry, and displayed the long knife in his hand.

He didn't have the chance to use it. Ki crow-hopped in and side-kicked the thug's wrist. The sharp cracking sound of bone breaking reached Ki's ears and the intruder, howling with pain, stepped back, grabbing for the holster at his waist with his other hand.

He managed to wrap his Remington pistol in his fingers and thumb back the hammer, but that was as far as he got. Spinning, Ki kicked again, his heel smashing into the man's face, shattering his nose. Blood streamed down the thug's face as his pistol clattered away and he fell over backward, clutching at his damaged face with both hands.

Doors opened down the hallway. Ki saw Ford, shirtless, gun in hand, step out into the hall, saw Jessie open her own door, and farther on excited darker faces peering into the hallway.

Ki reached down, took the thug under his arms, and dragged him into his own room. In a second Jessie was there, blanket around her bare shoulders.

"What have you got, Ki?" she asked. Ford was in the doorway, and behind him other hotel guests. Jessie nodded and Gleason shut the door in their faces, stepping in, thrusting his pistol into his belt as he stared down at the man with the damaged face. The thug continued to writhe on the floor, blood streaming through his fingers.

"I don't know, suppose we ask him who he is and who sent him here?" Ki answered.

Jessie crouched to look more closely at the man and as his mouth opened again with anguish she shook her head. "It won't do much good, Ki."

"Why not?" Ford asked.

"Someone has cut his tongue out," she answered with a grimace of disgust.

"The perfect assassin," Ki muttered. He had seen it before, in the Orient.

"I don't suppose he could write down who sent him," Ford suggested. He was watching the thug with awed fascination.

"We don't even know what language he speaks," Ki said. "Look at him—I don't think he's Mexican. Malaysian? Siamese? It's not usual to find a literate man from those parts of the world anyway. No. I think we can do little but let him go—unless we want to get involved with the local law, and to me that seems like a poor idea."

"Then we haven't learned a damn thing," Ford growled.

"Except that they know," Jessie amended. "They know that we are here and we know that they wish to kill us."

The man on the floor had risen slowly to a half-crouch, one hand braced behind him. Now he fled across the room and leaped from the window. They made no move to stop him—what was the good of it?

There was nothing left to do but return to their beds, to wait for morning. Ki stood at the window for a while, looking out at the dark sea, once seeing, or believing he did, a dark, ghostly frigate far away, gliding across the black waters.

★
Chapter 6

The fisherman's name was Miguel. He didn't offer his last name, nor did it matter. He had a boat and knew the local waters. Not long after daybreak, with the rising sun painting the sails of the small fisher red, they sailed out of the harbor at San Felipe, Miguel and his grandfather expertly handling the small craft as it wove its way through hundreds of other small boats.

The sun was brilliant on the water. Astern a huge batray swam away with amazing grace and speed.

"We are looking for an island where a ship might be sheltered," Jessie told Miguel.

"Not so many Señorita," Miguel answered. He held a shroud line and stood peering forward, weather-cut eyes dark in his tanned, lined face.

"But there are a few?"

"*Si,* San Tomas, Little San Tomas, maybe Viejas Island."

"This would be a large ship," Ford Gleason put in. The fisherman turned suddenly wary eyes to the soldier.

"Yes, Señor. A large ship, I know."

And Miguel did know. He knew it was a large ship because he knew what these three were looking for, the ship of the *pirata.* He didn't like this job, but there was gold in it, more than he and grandfather could make fishing in a month, and so Miguel had shrugged and taken on the job. Maybe he was as crazy as these three *norteamericanos* who went chasing the cutthroats of the gulf.

50

The ship canted away from the wind and Miguel leaned back, keeping his balance, guiding the boat toward the distant hillock-shaped island called San Tomas.

It was two hours out, the sun blistering, the water glassy, and the boat took another hour to sail completely around San Tomas, much taller than it had appeared from the shore, lifting its craggy head two hundred feet into the air.

"There," Gleason said, pointing. A harbor had opened up in the wall of stone, a narrow, deep cove where a ship could be hidden easily.

Miguel pointed out the rocky reef that slipped past their hull. "Difficult for a large ship to enter the harbor," he said.

"But not impossible?" Ki asked.

Miguel shrugged. "If the captain is very good."

"Take us in closer, Miguel, *por favor*," Jessie said and Miguel's eyes grew even more wary. He looked to his toothless grandfather, who made a gesture with his first two fingers and his thumb, rubbing them together.

Miguel said, "It is dangerous for my little boat, Señorita. If it is damaged, I have nothing."

Jessie silently slipped a gold coin into Miguel's palm and he magically became less concerned with the safety of his boat. The fisherman pulled again on his line and the little boat heeled over to port, slipping through a gap in the gray stone reef.

They sailed on more slowly; the rising bluffs cut the wind sharply. Far above they could see stunted trees, cedars perhaps, growing along the rim. There was no beach; the bluffs sloped steeply down and continued into the blue water.

"There's enough anchorage," Ki observed.

"It's deep enough," Jessie agreed, but there was no sign of the ship, no indication that anyone had ever used these shores to lay up on. There were no shacks, cleared areas, or signs of man-made habitation.

51

"No ship here," Miguel said, and there was relief in his voice.

"No, there's no ship."

"Still," Gleason said, "it's a possibility, isn't it? One worth remembering."

The inlet on Little San Tomas five miles distant was less sheltered, shallower, but it too was a possibility. "Is there fresh water?" Ki asked. "That's a primary need."

"Water, *si,*" Miguel answered, pointing to the uplands. "Springs high up, and on San Tomas as well. On Viejas, *quien sabe?*"

Viejas Island was the least promising of the three. It was dry, barren, and although the cove on the eastern shore was deep enough for a seagoing ship, there was no shelter from winds or prying eyes.

Sunbaked, weary, they sailed back toward San Felipe, Miguel whistling now that his fear of running into an armed pirate ship was gone. From a mile out they saw it.

"There it is," Ki said, pointing toward shore. "The *California,* a day early."

The packet ship from Los Angeles was still unfurling sail as they sailed past it and tied up at the dock. Jessie could see armed sailors patrolling the ship's deck.

They thanked Miguel, gave him twenty dollars more and on legs somewhat rubbery strolled down the rotting planks of the dock to the *California.*

A sailor in a worn peacoat stood at the foot of the gang- way with a rifle in the crook of his arm.

"No one goes aboard," he told them.

"Lieutenant Ford Gleason, U.S. Army," Gleason said, showing his identification. "Those are army goods you're carrying."

The seaman was dubious. Gleason was out of uniform; the other two sure as hell weren't soldiers. Finally he let them pass. "The captain's for'd. Main hatch."

"Who is your captain?" Jessie asked. The sailor paused for a moment before he answered, letting his eyes comb this blonde mermaid.

"Drew. Factor Drew," he answered finally.

"Factor Drew," Jessie said with some pleasure. "Good."

"You know him, Jessie?" Gleason asked.

"I've met him. He used to work for my father."

"Your father?" the seaman asked, his forehead furrowing. "God love us—is your name Starbuck, miss?"

"It is. Jessica Starbuck."

The sailor made a half-salute. "I worked for your father too then. Alex Starbuck. Out of Yokohama on the *Lady Light*. My name's Henderson, I don't suppose Alex Starbuck ever mentioned me."

"Yes, of course he did, many times," Jessie said. It was a lie, but it cost her nothing and brightened the sailor's eyes.

"They tell me he's dead. Sorry, miss."

"Thank you. The forward hatch, you say?"

"Yes, miss, that's right," the sailor said and he stepped aside to let them pass, his eyes alive with appreciation and nostalgia.

They found Factor Drew, arms behind his back, silently watching his crew bring the army cargo up onto the *California*'s deck. He was hawk-faced, balding beneath his captain's cap, gray-eyed, and sun-browned. He turned slowly as Jessica Starbuck and the men approached, puzzlement giving way to surprise and pleasure.

"Jessie! Damn all!" He took her hands. "What in God's name is Jessica Starbuck doing in Mexico?"

"Looking into this business," she answered.

"The piracy. . ." Drew dropped her hands, tipping back his hat to show a little more of his scalp. "It's Starbuck money in this?"

"No. The army needed a little unofficial help. They can't come south to protect their shipments."

"And so you . . . ?" Drew shook his head. He had known Alex Starbuck well, had met Jessie as a girl, but he couldn't picture this daughter of the old man as a warrior. The man with her he knew was a warrior. "Ki, isn't it?

53

We've never met, but I know about you," he said, extending a hand.

His eyes shifted to Gleason. "We haven't met."

"This," Jessie said, "is Lieutenant Ford Gleason, U.S. Army. Detached," she added with a smile.

"Army, are you? Well, as you see, we've done our bit. I expect the steamer you've contracted will be in come morning. We caught some stiff southeasterlies above Guadalajara and came in a day ahead."

"The steamer will be on its way down from Yuma?" Ki asked.

"That's right. The *President Grant*. I understand she's already been taken once by the pirates."

"That's Captain Easley's boat," Gleason said. "He's got guts, it seems."

"Meantime," Drew went on, "I'm keeping a guard on this cargo. I'm not going to lose it to *anyone*."

"Captain," Ki said, "do you mind if we sleep aboard your vessel tonight?"

"Sleep aboard?" Drew frowned briefly. "No, I suppose not. Figure you can do a better job at watching our cargo than I can?"

"It's not that. We want to be here in the morning when the *President Grant* arrives, and—there has been some trouble ashore."

"Oh?" The frown deepened.

"Someone tried to kill Jessie last night," Gleason explained.

"Then you'll sleep aboard. I'll have my first officer move out of his cabin. That'll do for you men. Jessie can have my cabin. I'll bunk with the second."

"It's really not necessary..." Jessie began to protest, but the captain shut her off.

"Nonsense. It's necessary if it's for your well-being. For you and for your father, rest his soul, I'd sail Shanghai waters blindfolded, Miss Starbuck."

Drew turned sharply as a crate of cargo was dropped, yelled a word of caution to his sailors, and said, "If you don't mind me asking, just what is it you three think you can do to keep the pirates from striking again, lifting this cargo as they have the others?"

"That," Jessie said, "is something we're going to talk about later, Captain Drew. I have an idea or two. Whether they'll work, I don't know."

"Bloody bastards," the captain said, adding a quick apology for his language, "I don't like pirates, no matter the sea. If I had guns aboard..." But he didn't and the company he worked for wouldn't have liked him risking the *California* in a sea battle if he had. Those days were gone for Drew and his eyes seemed to reflect knowledge of that fact. Time passed; men grew older. He no longer ran a fully armed schooner out of Yokohama, ready to do battle with Oriental pirates.

"The pirate leader," Ki said, "is a tall dark man with earrings. He must have some background in this sort of work. Have you any idea who he could be, Captain Drew?"

"From the description, half a hundred," Drew answered. "Odd place for a privateer to show up, though. You'd almost think the man would have to know the army's inside plans."

Gleason looked at Jessie. He didn't like to think that was what was happening. He preferred to believe that chance was at work here. That eyes and ears in San Felipe had become aware of what was happening and somehow the captain of the pirate vessel had gotten the word.

It seemed to be stretching chance even to a man who wanted to believe in it.

Ki had seen the movement along the forward rail and his eyes had automatically shifted that way. He was a hunter, a wary man, expecting almost anything at any time. He had survived this long by living that way.

He hadn't expected to see what he saw now.

The two women were beautiful, especially the taller one, sleek and sexually enticing in an artless—or seemingly artless—way. She wore black, a black-lace veil over

55

her dark hair, black dress reaching to the deck, high tor-
toiseshell comb in the intricate knot her hair formed at the
base of her skull. She moved and gestured with grace as
she pointed toward the sea, laughed once softly, and turned
her back to the rail to look at Ki—or past him—as her
companion looked toward the distant islands.

It was Jessie who asked, *"Who* is that?" Ki had made an
effort to keep from staring but his eyes had their own will,
it seemed.

"Who?" Captain Drew glanced toward the rail. "Oh,
that one. Angelina Guiterrez is her name. Other one's her
cousin, Rosa. Nice-looking ladies, aren't they?"

Ki seemed definitely to be in agreement with Factor
Drew's observation. No one could much blame him. The
woman was even more beautiful than her portrait. A Spanish aristocrat with doe eyes capable of darting, fiery
glances, pale skin with lustrous black hair, high-breasted,
svelte, and graceful.

"The governor's daughter," Gleason said.

"Is she? I knew she was something," Drew said. "You
can always tell the old blood, the old money."

"She doesn't want to go ashore here?" Ki asked.

"Says she's waiting for the steamboat, something about
surprising her father." The ship's captain shrugged. "Whatever she likes is fine by me."

"Guiterrez said she was in Alta California, visiting. I
wonder if he knows she's on board the *California?"* Jessie
said.

"Don't see how." Drew looked at the woman again,
perhaps recalling his younger days. "They came aboard
minutes before we sailed. Sudden notion, it seemed. Little
black carriage brought them onto the dock. The lady seems
whimsical, but..." He didn't have to complete the sen-
tence. She was beautiful, no matter how spoiled or whimsical she might be.

It was growing dark already and Factor Drew signaled
to his crew to knock off for the day. "I hope you'll all dine
with me tonight," he said to Jessie. "I've sent ashore for

some fresh provisions. My cook is something of an artist."
He glanced at Ki. "Señorita Guiterrez and her cousin will
be present."

"Not that it matters," Gleason said.

Ki bowed from the neck. "It will be an honor to share
your table, Captain—and to make the acquaintance of the
young ladies."

"It might be an honor to meet them," Drew said, "but
maybe not much of a pleasure. That Angelina Guiterrez
treats just about everyone as her servant, myself included."

"Nevertheless," Ki began, but he never completed his
thought. His eyes returned to the young Spanish woman
and stayed there until Jessie nudged him.

"Before dinner I want to talk to you in private, Captain
Drew," she said.

"Go ahead," Factor Drew said.

Jessie looked at the crew climbing from the hold, walking forward, joking, planning a night ashore perhaps. "No,
not here. I mean very privately."

"My cabin then," Drew said, looking puzzled.

His cabin was forward, all brass and mahogany, sextant
on the table pressing down a chart recognizable as the gulf
and its islands.

Drew pulled out his chair and sat down, taking a bottle
of peppermint schnapps from his drawer, offering it
around. Ki and Jessie refused, Gleason indicated a small
portion with his thumb and forefinger and was served.

"Now then," Drew asked, leaning back, "what's so secret?"

"Is there any way to contact the *President Grant?*" Jessie asked. She was looking out the porthole, watching the
sky redden.

"Tonight?" Drew asked in surprise. He spread his
hands. "Not without swimming. Unless Easley ties up at
Cordoba overnight."

"Would he be likely to do that?"

Drew pondered it. "Maybe. I might if I was running a
paddleboat. Don't like to get them in deep water much.

Seas might rise. He's running empty with no fear of pirates. Yes, he might."

"How far is that?" Jessie asked.

"Thirty miles. It would be a decent night port if he's on schedule for our morning meet."

"I don't want to meet him in the morning," Jessie said, turning to face the cabin. "I want it to be tonight."

"Tonight?"

"And not here. At sea."

"That's not so easily done," Drew said. "Easley hasn't been contacted, I've got my sails furled, half my men ashore."

"It's essential," Jessie insisted.

"Essential, is it?" Drew repeated, drinking his liquor.

"Yes, it is. The pirates know your schedule. They know exactly when the *President Grant* will be loaded and ready to steam up the gulf. It's a simple matter for them to intercept this shipment as they have all the others."

Drew was silent, turning his glass. Peppermint and alcohol hung in the air. "You know, Jessie, I've done what my company asked me to do. I've fulfilled our contract by delivering this consignment to San Felipe. You're asking me on my own initiative, risking both the goods and my ship, to sail to a rendezvous with Easley in the dead of night."

"I know that, Captain Drew. As for the money involved . . ."

Drew waved a hand. "The money isn't the issue, Jessie. I have no confidence that we can even intercept Easley, have you?"

"We can try. If, as you speculate, he's tied up at Cordoba, then we should be able to rendezvous before dawn."

"How do we contact him?"

"One of us rides all night," Jessie said. The idea was stuck in her head and no one was going to get it out. "If you could find a location, mark it on the chart, I'll do it myself. A pair of fast horses . . ."

"I will go if anyone goes, Jessie," Ki said quietly and

58

she hesitated a minute before nodding.

"It will give us a chance, don't you see," Jessie went on. "No one will know where or when the goods are being transferred. The pirates won't be just sitting out there watching for the *President Grant*."

Drew removed his cap and rubbed his balding head vigorously. "I'd have to bring my crew back. The word would get around that something was up."

"Something, but they still wouldn't know what or where."

"Miss Starbuck," the captain said with a hollow sigh, "if you weren't who you are and I didn't owe your father for so many past favors—risk my cargo and my ship, sail unknown waters in the dead of night—"

"You'll do it then," Jessie said.

"Yes." Drew sighed again. "I'll do it." He pushed the brass sextant from his chart and studied the coastline and the islands of the gulf. "Perhaps if we could meet the steamer . . ."

Ki held up a hand and put his finger to his lips. The others glanced at the door as Ki moved on cat feet toward it. There was someone out there, listening.

Ki put his hand on the brass door handle and yanked it open, and a very surprised-looking Angelina Guiterrez said, "Good evening, Captain. I did not know you had guests. What time is dinner tonight? Rosa and I must dress."

The woman had regained her composure instantly. Now she swept into the room, dark skirts trailing, nodding to Gleason and Jessie. She circled the captain's table, her hand resting negligently on the chart where Drew had penciled an X lightly.

"Dinner will be at eight, Señorita," Drew said.

"Bueno, gracias," she replied. "And your friends will join us?" Her eyes went to Ki, lingered there, and danced away.

"Yes, they will join us," Drew answered.

"So then," she said in her deeply accented English, "we

will be expecting you all there." Her dark eyes flashed once more to Ki's and then she swept out of the cabin, imperious, erect.

Ki closed the door behind her. "You said she is planning to go north on the *President Grant* with her cousin to surprise her father," he said to Factor Drew. "Doesn't she know anything about the pirates?"

"She's been told. Try convincing that one of anything."

"It's a shame," Jessie said to Ki, "that you won't be able to make dinner after all."

"A shame," Ki said, mostly to himself. "The lady seemed quite interesting."

"You'll need this," Drew said, rolling up the chart and handing it to Ki, "and some luck."

"Some luck and some fast horses."

Ki folded the chart and tucked it inside his vest. Then there was nothing left to do but wait until full dark. Drew called his second mate and issued an order to bring the crew back on board. The mate was surprised but didn't question the order.

When it was dark enough Ki left the cabin, slipped to the side of the ship, and to the dock, landing softly. Rising, he looked around carefully. Then he was off through the night, heading for the stable where their horses were being kept. Eyes watched him go and before Ki had ridden out of San Felipe there were men trailing him, men who meant to make sure that Ki did not live out the night.

★
Chapter 7

Dinner was at eight and the two Spanish women came in regally as always, Angelina in white satin and white veil, her cousin more sedate in dark blue. Both women were beautiful, although Rosa's mouth was a bit too generous, her body more compact than the sleek Angelina's. Diamond rings and necklaces flashing, they moved royally across the room and were seated by the captain, who wore his dress uniform.

Jessie had her traveling clothes on, and being at the same table with the two Spanish women should have intimidated her, would have intimidated most women, but Jessica Starbuck was supremely confident of her own attractiveness, of her place in life. She had dresses at home to match any these two could import from Paris and she liked to wear them, but Jessie didn't *need* them.

Gleason didn't seem to impress the ladies either. His boyish good looks and outdoor cut apparently didn't appeal to them. Angelina's eyes roved the cabin, however, and she asked, "Where is your other friend? The tall one?"

"Ki decided to eat ashore," Jessie said as she seated herself and smiled across the table at Angelina, whose dark eyes sparked with disbelief. There was a man who would rather dine alone ashore than eat with her?

The look passed quickly. Drew's cook came in with roast pork garnished with orange slices and parsley. Angelina looked at it without much interest as the captain carved.

Rosa asked timidly, "Captain? It is permitted to go ashore?" Her eyelids blinked furiously. "If your friend is gone? I understood the passengers were to stay on the ship. Why I do not know."

"Ki is not a passenger."

"Then it is not permitted to go ashore?"

"There has been some trouble in town," Drew said easily. "It's not safe for you."

Rosa just blinked more furiously. Angelina, taking a sliver of pork on the tine of her fork and touching it to her pink tongue, said, "We will have no trouble reaching our destination, Captain?"

"None at all." Under his breath he said, "I hope."

"Then it does not matter. What is there to see in San Felipe? My cousin is simply tired of being on a boat."

"It's a long journey," Gleason said. Angelina's eyes focused on him as if with surprise.

"Yes. Have you had a long journey as well?" she asked Jessie.

Jessie put her knife and fork down briefly. "Ki and I have just arrived from Texas."

"Texas? Then you are a cowgirl, perhaps," Angelina said, her gaze scouring Jessie, the beautiful face, green eyes, fine uplifted breasts, the simple green skirt and jacket of her traveling clothes.

"Yes, a cowgirl," Jessie said, picking up her fork again.

"How very . . . nice," Angelina said. The door opened again and her eyes went that way. The cook was obviously not the man she had been hoping to see there. "Ki, your friend," Angelina said, leaning forward slightly so that her breasts were more fully displayed, firm, white breasts decorated with diamonds, "is he a . . . *vaquero?*"

"Something like that," Jessie answered. "He is a very important man in Texas," she added, pleasing Angelina.

Gleason glanced sideways at Jessie, shook his head slightly, and returned to the pork roast, which he and Drew were having no trouble putting down.

Abovedecks they could hear movement now, men

crossing the deck, a muffled shout, the creak of a boom being brought into place. Angelina looked up, startled.

"And what is this?" she asked.

"Preparing to sail," Drew told her.

"To sail! Now?"

"Going to catch the night tradewinds," Drew said and Jessie lifted an eyebrow. Angelina accepted that but was puzzled.

"But the steamboat to take us home?"

"She's had engine trouble. We can either wait an extra day or go up and meet her at Cordoba. I've decided to sail on to Cordoba."

"But, Captain . . ."

"I wouldn't want you ladies to be late," Drew said with a smile. "After all, I promised you would reach home on time."

"Oh, then, that is fine," Angelina said. She began to eat with more concentration. She didn't challenge the captain's explanation. It was easy for her to accept the fact that the ship was sailing just so she wouldn't be inconvenienced. She had lived her life accepting that all would always be as she wanted.

Spoiled. Jessie watched the woman eat. Spoiled, but there was no denying her beauty. No wonder Ki had eyes for her. Hard to handle, this Angelina Guiterrez, Jessie estimated, but then if any man could handle her, it would be Ki. Ki, Jessie thought confidently, could handle almost anything.

Ki could have used some of that confidence himself just then. The rifle shot from out of the darkness had struck his horse in the neck and the animal, panicked and in pain, had leaped from the trail over the fifty-foot bluff to Ki's left and plummeted down to the water below as Ki kicked free of the stirrups and flung himself wildly to the ground, crawling into the chia and sagebrush as the rifle spoke again, kicking up dirt in the *te* master's face.

Ki rolled into deeper cover, eyes scouring the hillside

above him. He saw nothing. There had only been the muzzle flash from the darkness and Ki hadn't had time to fix the gunman's position in his mind.

Wait then. Be still, watch and wait. He was still watching the slope when the second sniper fired a shot from behind Ki, the bullet clipping brush near Ki's head.

He pressed himself flat against the ground and began to crawl, needing to change his own position before one of those bullets found its mark.

The guns were silent again. Ki clung to the earth, his hand slipping inside his vest pocket to remove two deadly *shuriken*. A tiny sound turned his head. A foot softly moving across the earth, snapping a tiny twig. That was one of them, then, but where was the second gunman?

Ki held himself ready, stilling his breath. He could see his remaining horse, the gray Jessie had been riding, standing on the trail, head hanging, looking content to wait as its owner played deadly man-games.

The hunter came on cautiously, rifle cocked and ready. The area Ki had hidden in was small, very small, with only a thin covering of brush. The stars were lost in the haze above him, making the night dark enough to be an ally, but not dark enough to protect him forever.

The man was within a few yards of Ki now, slowly surveying the brush. He was near enough to kill, but Ki knew that his first movement might be his last if the second sniper spotted him.

The throwing star was cool in his hand, familiar and deadly. Still Ki hesitated until he saw the searcher's eyes widen slightly, saw his head start to turn toward where Ki lay concealed.

The *shuriken* sang from Ki's hand, thudding into flesh as it imbedded itself in the eye of the stalker. Ki was up and moving instantly, weaving as he ran, bullets tagging at his heels as the second sniper opened fire.

Ki spotted a shallow ditch and flung himself into it to lay panting, watching. After a while a soft whistle sounded to his left, but there was no answering whistle. The other sniper was dead.

Ki waited a while, trying to locate the other man, but he was good, this one, and very cautious now that his friend was down. Ki lifted his head slightly and looked along the ditch, cut by run-off water and sloping down toward the bluff, which broke away sharply.

He started down the gulley, staying low, his elbows pulling him over the broken ground. Near the bluff where Ki's eyes were fixed the brush was thicker and there were a few broken trees, enough to conceal movement. If he could reach there, perhaps circle back toward the lone horse . . .

The sniper was suddenly over him, eyes gleaming. Ki's hand snaked out and hooked the ambusher's heels. The rifle in the man's hand touched off, so near Ki's face that he felt momentary searing heat.

The sniper fell hard, rifle clattering free, the breath escaping from his lungs with a *whoosh*. He wore a handgun and he went for that now, a savage curse frothing from his lips. He never got the gun out.

Ki's hand shot out with the deadly speed of a sidewinder, twisting as it landed in the V formed by the sniper's ribs. The *choku-zuki* thrust stopped the thug's heart instantly and he could only gape at Ki as his finger twitched on the butt of his Colt revolver, as useless now as his cold dead hands.

Ki rose slowly, wiping back his dark hair. In a half-crouch he carefully swept the area with his eyes once more, not wanting to chance the presence of a third man.

The night was still except for the lapping of the sea at the base of the bluffs and the startled hoot of an owl, and Ki started back toward his horse at a jog-trot. The night was short and he had a long way to ride yet.

If the *President Grant* wasn't docked at Cordoba then all of this was for nothing, but still, Jessie had been right —they had to try something.

The horse was worn to a nub by the time Ki reached the

small coastal pueblo and Ki was well behind schedule. Losing the other horse had slowed him down considerably. It was close to three-thirty in the morning when he found the squalid collection of docks and fishers and, tied at the end of a long pier, the *President Grant*.

Ki looked warily at the ancient, waterlogged dock and swung from his horse, leaving it tied to an upright. He moved quickly and quietly down the dock to where the steamboat sat motionless on a dark sea.

"Just stand steady there," a voice from aboard the boat said, and Ki saw a man with a shotgun standing at the bow.

"I want to see Captain Easley," Ki said.

"Easley's sleeping and he don't hire nobody on at this time of night. Why don't you just be on your way."

"It's army business," Ki persisted and the man on the boat peered down at him.

"Don't see no brass buttons on your shirt, mister."

"Look, this is urgent. Really."

"What in hell's all the bluster!" a bulky figure pulling dark trousers over white longjohns bellowed.

"Man says he wants to see you, Captain, says it's official army business, real important."

"Army." A long silence followed that grunted word. "All right. Send him on up. You walk along behind him with that scattergun, though."

"Yes, sir." He nodded to Ki. "You heard the man, didn't you?"

Ki went up the gangway and was taken to the captain's cabin. Easley sat dourly on his bunk, hair sticking up every which way, eyes red. "Can't get no sleep no matter what I try," he said. The red eyes lifted suddenly to Ki's face. "What kind of crap is this, you ain't army."

"I am Ki," he responded.

"That one, are you?"

"You know him, Captain?" the man with the shotgun asked incredulously.

"I know of him. Thaddeus York at the post said some kind of Chinaman and some woman was down here . . ."

66

The captain's eyes narrowed shrewdly. "With an army officer. You know his name, don't you?"

"Yes," Ki responded. "We are down here with Lieutenant Ford Gleason. Now, please, Captain Easley, can we get down to business? There isn't much time."

"Time? Time for what?" the captain asked, rising.

And Ki told him.

Easley just stood shaking his head, not liking a bit of it. He looked from Ki to the window where night still hung and then back. "It's crazy," he announced finally.

"It's about our only chance of pulling one over on the pirates," Ki insisted. "The *California* is already under way, making for the spot on that chart. What can it cost you, Captain Easley, to sail early and rendezvous with the ship tonight?"

"Sleep," Easley growled. "Or a collision at sea. Let me see that damn chart again." He studied it, the frown on his face turning his mouth down sharply.

"Don't sound right to me, Captain," the sailor said, but Easley waved a silencing hand at him.

Finally he lifted his eyes to Ki. "I don't want to meet up with those pirates again, Ki. Look at what happened to the *Mas Mal*. Blown out of the water and her master with it." He sighed long and hard and then agreed, "All right. I'll chance it. Doran," he said to the sailor, "roust the helmsman and the crew. Issue arms as well. Break out all the lanterns you can muster. We'll need plenty of light out there.

"You, mister," he told Ki, leveling a stubby finger, "you had better be on the up-and-up. You're sailing with us and if any damn thing at all goes wrong, you'll be the first to feel it."

"I understand," Ki replied quietly.

"All right, then—damn all, where's my shirt?"

Ki went up on deck, the captain's still-cautious eyes following him. Ki understood Easley. He had been burned once and only his strong desire to beat the pirates overcame his fear of being burned again. Ki was aware of being

67

watched on the deck, but he paid no attention to it. He leaned on the rail, watched the half-asleep sailors cast off lines and move grumbling about the deck. When the boilers were fired up it was a sudden shock against the stillness of the night. Lamps flickered on along the shore and a few curious villagers emerged to watch.

It took Easley fifteen minutes to get a head of steam up and yank the lever that put the great paddlewheels in motion. Water flew up on either side of the *Grant,* filling the night air with mist.

They backed from the dock and slowly the ponderous steamer turned, making its way out onto the silky, starlit waters of the gulf. Ki's guard left him, figuring that no one in his right mind was going to leap overboard after clearing port, and the *te* master walked to the bow rail to watch the sea, the stars, to watch for approaching sails—friendly or pirate.

Easley found him there. The captain had his coat buttoned crookedly, his hands thrust in his trouser pockets. "Might work," the sailing man admitted, leaning beside Ki. "With a little luck, it just might work. Too damned bad we have to have lights to load by—it's a dark night. The bastards'd never find us out here.

"Tell me," he asked, "do they know the *California*'s leaving port?"

"They do by now," Ki answered.

"Still . . . finding us won't be that easy. It just, damn me, might work."

Then he shambled away, walking up the steps to the wheelhouse, where a bleary-eyed pilot stared out at the night, aiming toward a spot on the empty sea represented by a pencil mark on his chart.

It was five o'clock when Ki spotted sail against the starlight. He turned to see if Easley had seen it as well. The captain's posture, leaning far forward, arms braced, indicated that he had, and in another moment the lights in the wheelhouse were extinguished and the two dark ships sailed on toward each other.

"Three-master!" someone above called and the lights in the wheelhouse went back on. It wasn't the pirate frigate then. It was the *California*.

Ki waited at the rail, watching as the sailing ship grew larger and more distinct. He lifted his eyes from time to time, searching the night sea as far as his vision allowed. There was no sign of the other ship, the one carrying cannon and saber-armed men.

They just might get away with this.

It was close to dawn, however, too close. The ambush Ki had fallen into had slowed the rendezvous. The lights in the wheelhouse blinked off and then on again three times and Easley cut his engines, letting the *Grant* drift to a stop before twin anchors were dropped, and she waited patiently for the arrival of the sleek schooner.

The *California* knifed through the water, dropped sail, and slowly swung in beside the *Grant*, not an easy maneuver for a sailing vessel, but Factor Drew knew his ship and his crew.

"Grappling hooks!" someone on board the *California* called. "Stand by, *President Grant*." Fenders, like those used in the Orient—burlap sacks filled with crushed coconut shells—were dropped from the rail of the *California* to hang suspended on long ropes, protecting the schooner's hull.

Grappling hooks arced through the air, and the lines on them were secured by the crew of the *Grant*. Slowly the two ships mated, the much taller *California* secured to the *Grant*. A gangway was fixed hastily and Factor Drew, followed by Jessie and Ford Gleason, made their way to the *Grant*'s deck.

"Made it, by God!" Easley said, showing some enthusiasm for the project now. "DeWitt, Henley, get that cargo moving. Any way you can. Damn the holds, we'll carry it on deck if we have to."

"Captain," Factor Drew said, and he offered Easley a very unmilitary salute, which Easley returned. "Congratulate your pilot. Quite a job in the dark."

"I will." Easley beamed. He nodded to Jessie and shook hands with Gleason, whom he knew. Work was in progress and moving rapidly. The *California* had had most of her cargo abovedecks and the combined crew was moving it swiftly to the *Grant*. "Captain," Easley said to Drew, "it couldn't be that you would consent to share a drink with me?"

"A drink?"

"Peppermint schnapps?" And Easley had his man. He started to lead Drew away to his cabin, but the sudden silence caused him to pause and look up the long plank walk. Not a man on either crew moved for a minute as the two Spanish ladies made their way delicately down the hazardous gangway to the deck of the *President Grant*.

"Your passengers," Drew said to the captain of the *Grant*.

"Holy . . . welcome," Easley said, catching himself. "For Yuma?"

"My father is Governor Alfredo Guiterrez," Angelina said. "We will expect you to deliver us to the beach below our hacienda." And with that the lady was gone, her cousin trailing after her.

"And," Factor Drew said quietly, "you are welcome to them. A drink, you said, Captain?"

"Yeah—" Easley was still staring after the women. "Keep that cargo moving, damn all, Henley!"

Ford Gleason stepped aside as the pair of sailors toting a crate filled with repeating rifles for use against Heart staggered down the gangplank. Jessie took his hand and squeezed it and Gleason put his arm around her waist, pulling her to him.

"You're going to beat them, Jessie. This time you're going to beat them."

"How long until dawn?" she asked.

"Maybe forty-five minutes. Not long, but they'll never find us."

"Let's hope not."

"Where's Ki? I wonder if he ran into any trouble."

"He made it, that's all that matters. As to where he is—" Jessie nodded her head forward. Señorita Angelina Guiterrez had surrounded him and Ki didn't seem to be minding it a bit. Rosa stood discreetly aside as Angelina, apparently scolding Ki, waved a finger at him.

"Poor bastard." Gleason laughed.

"You think so, do you?" Jessie asked.

"All I mean is that I prefer them blonde and American," Ford Gleason said and he turned to her, hugging her to him until she could feel his manhood rising enthusiastically.

"Wrong time, wrong place, Ford," she said.

"There will be other times, Jessie."

"Yes," she said promisingly, looking into his eyes, "there will be many other times."

"When we get to Yuma."

"*If* we get to Yuma."

"We'll get there," the army lieutenant said with more passion than Jessie expected. "We have to."

"This is really important to you, isn't it, Ford? More important than you've told me. Is it the promotion?"

He laughed, but it was a bitter expression. "The promotion, no. Nor Thaddeus York's ass. It is," he said, turning to lean on the rail," something that is *necessary*. Yuma is dying. This damned Águila Rojas and Heart combined are killing a good town. They aren't fighting for any cause, not for their people or their land, but only to profit, and they don't care what has to be done to profit. Heart is a butcher. He's better equipped than the army. Those crates you saw coming down that gangplank are going to make a difference."

There was fire in his voice and anger in his eyes. Jessie asked, "What happened, Ford?"

"What happened? All right, I'll tell you. A little settlement south of us, a place called Trinidad where no one ever went or cared to go. There was nothing there but five Mexican families scratching at the earth, trying to bring in a corn crop and raise a few chickens. Rojas went there, demanding food and money. The people of Trinidad had nothing to give him and his men—and so he butchered them all, men, women, children. We weren't there to stop him because we were chasing Heart up along Little Butte. Little Butte, where he cut off a patrol and massacred six soldiers. One of them was a friend of mine. One was my brother."

"I'm sorry, Ford," was all Jessie could say.

"Then these damned pirates happen along and we can't even supply our people with ammunition." He lifted his eyes to the empty sea. "It is *necessary*, Jessie. Necessary to rid this part of the country of all of these people who think they're so far away from civilization that nothing can touch them, that they have no rules they have to live by.

"It is," he repeated with a heavy shrug, *"necessary."*

The sky was beginning to gray in the east before the crews had finished shifting the cargo from the *California* to the *Grant*. By that time Drew and Captain Easley had finished their drinks and both looked eager to be going.

Factor Drew said, "It was wonderful seeing you again, Jessie. But I hope we don't meet again soon—under these circumstances."

"You were enormously helpful," Jessie said, taking the seaman's hands. "My father would have appreciated it. I appreciate it."

"Nothing to it. Don't pay any attention to me—I'd delight in seeing you again under any circumstances, in a pit filled with tigers." He took her hands, kissed her cheek lightly, saluted Easley again with that peculiar wave of the hand and trudged up the plank to his own ship.

Ki was beside Gleason now, Angelina clinging to him with her eyes while Rosa gaped. The gangway was pulled up, the lines untied, and the sails of the *California* began to be hoisted again.

The boilers of the *President Grant* were fired up as the schooner began to catch the morning breeze and sail away into the rising sun. Easley, perspiring slightly, said, "Thank God. It's over."

72

"Just beginning, I'm afraid," Ki said. "Look."

All eyes followed his pointing finger, and they saw it too. A sailing ship on the horizon, closing fast. A four-masted frigate.

★
Chapter 8

The pirate ship had the wind in her sails and she seemed to fairly skim across the water, closing distance rapidly as the *California* heeled to starboard and the ungainly steamboat, the *President Grant,* stubbornly, slowly turned to make a run toward the mouth of the Colorado, where no deep-hulled sailing vessel could hope to follow.

Easley strangled on a dark oath and rushed toward the wheelhouse, shouting for his men to be armed with rifles. Ki and Jessie simply stood and watched the black frigate closing. There wasn't a hell of a lot else to do.

"Can we outrun it?" Angelina asked. Her eyes, oddly, did not show fear, only a sort of challenge. Ki answered her.

"Not if she keeps on at that speed. It must be seven miles to the Colorado. She'll cut across our bows and stop us."

"Then we will fight," the Spanish woman said with determination, and Jessie looked at Angelina with new appreciation.

"We won't fight cannon with rifles," Ki told her.

Rosa began inching away along the rail as if by being fifteen or twenty feet farther away she would be safe. Ford Gleason's face was intent with much the same sort of emotion Angelina had articulated. He wanted to fight, wanted very much to meet this pirate king with sabers or pistols or empty hands.

"Look!" Angelina's hand went up excitedly. "What is he doing?"

He was the captain of the *California,* for Factor Drew had brought his schooner about and was now running directly toward the pirate ship.

"Suicide," Gleason muttered appreciatively. "Why?"

"To give us a chance," Jessie said.

"And lose his ship?"

"They won't be expecting it," Ki pointed out. "They won't have their cannon ready. He just wants the pirates to change course, to lose the wind from their sails. If they are forced to turn it could bring them up almost dead in the water."

"If they don't have cannon ready aboard that frigate," Gleason said, glancing at Jessie.

"We owe that man something," Jessie said. "Whether it works or not, we owe Factor Drew."

They could only watch as the paddlewheeler, steam valves wide open, throttle to full ahead, struggled across the gulf toward the mouth of the Colorado River.

The *California* was quicker and as the frigate tried to evade her, Factor Drew's smaller ship changed tack smartly and continued on across the pirate ship's bow. They heard the distant popping of small-arms fire and then the horrible, heavier sound of a starboard cannon from the pirate vessel. Smoke curled from a single gunport and then there was no more firing as the *California* cut off the angle of fire.

She sailed straight across the bow of the dark frigate and Ki, holding his breath without realizing it, grinned as he saw sail drop on the pirate ship, saw her cut hard to starboard. The *California* sailed straight on past, turning into the wind now to avoid any port cannon that might have been readied.

And then the frigate was dead in the water, the *California* sailing away to the south, one parting, misjudged cannonball striking the water, far, far astern of Drew's vessel.

75

"Give her steam, Captain," Gleason shouted, raising a joyous fist, "all you've got!"

Easley didn't respond. He didn't hear the army lieutenant and he was already busy doing just what Gleason had urged him to do. Behind them the frigate came slowly around, her sails filling with wind once more, but the *President Grant* was drawing away.

Astonishingly, Angelina let out a shout of victory, a loud cheer that suggested that the blood of the conquistadores was not dead in her veins. She turned to the others, shrugged, and leaned placidly on the rail to watch, moving closer to Ki until her hips were touching his.

"He's got the wind," Gleason said. Then he turned to look toward the northern shore, where the mouth of the Colorado remained hidden behind the sea haze. Angelina didn't even glance shoreward as they steamed on past her father's great casa. No matter, there was no way in hell Easley was going to stop to let his passengers off now. The captain of the *Grant* had one goal in mind, only one—beat the pirates, beat them to the Colorado, where his shallow boat could steam on to Yuma, leaving the big cannon-carrying deep-water vessel behind.

The boilers hissed and stuttered, the paddlewheels churned, spinning fans of water into the bright sky above the deep-blue gulf.

The frigate was closing.

One cannonball arced through the air, falling short of the *Grant*'s stern by a hundred feet, but that had only been a range finder and a warning. Easley didn't even look back—they weren't going to beat him this time.

Ahead now he saw it—the mouth of the glorious, beautiful red Colorado River flowing into the deep-blue water of the gulf—and he turned to lift a defiant hand toward the pirate frigate, a gesture that was cut off short as a second ball, this one better aimed, splashed into the water within fifteen feet of the steamer's vulnerable hull.

Sailors lined the rails and began firing with small arms, but what damage they could do to the pirate ship was beyond Jessie. She only stood and watched, swiveling her head from the frigate to the mouth of the Colorado and back, silently urging Easley on, knowing that he knew better than any of them how to wrench speed from his flatboat.

"We're going to make it. By God, we're going to make it," Ford Gleason said, and then the cannonball struck the port side of the wheelhouse and the steamboat seemed to slough away, dipping out from under them. Jessie went to her knees and gripped the rail. There was a gaping, smoking hole in the wheelhouse, some flames rising from the white-painted walls.

Ki heard Angelina scream and he spun toward her, seeing her face go rigid, pale, seeing her arm uplifted, pointing behind them where a human figure in blue drifted toward the frigate.

"Rosa!" she shrieked. "It's Rosa, stop the boat! Go back for my cousin!"

She rushed toward the wheelhouse and Ki had to drag her down. She fell flailing, scratching, proving that her schooling hadn't all been in a convent as an extensive vocabulary of Spanish curses bubbled from her pretty red lips.

"We can't do anything about it," Ki said.

"*Estúpido!* Stupid cowboy, stupid ship captain, stop the boat, go back. That is Rosa!"

"He can't stop now. Even if he could, he wouldn't! The rest of us might end up dead."

"Stupid, stupid, stupid!" she shouted and she pounded on Ki's back with her fists. Then she was crying, face buried against his chest as the *Grant* steamed on and the dark frigate continued to close.

"He'll have to turn back soon," Ford said to Jessie. "He can't risk tearing her bottom out. We're nearly to the river mouth."

But the frigate showed no signs of stopping. It seemed to hover over them, yellow-white canvas stark against the bright morning sky.

"We're in," Ford breathed. "Into the river."

Jessie glanced down. The water was muddy-red. Beside them red desert rolled away to the interior. Ahead bluffs rose to the blue sky.

"Goddamn him," Ford breathed, "he's coming after us."

And it was true. The frigate's captain, with seeming disregard for his ship, had entered the river and was still closing. "It's insane," Jessie said. "He'll wreck it. He must know."

Whether he knew or not the captain of the frigate kept coming, all sail hoisted as he pursued the little steamer. As Jessie watched the frigate lurched, perhaps striking a sandbar, and then came suddenly broadside.

Gunports snapped open and cannon fired from eight portals, filling the air with smoke and screaming cannonballs that whistled through the air, two of them striking the *Grant,* momentarily causing it to falter. But the damage was superficial and the steamboat chugged on, leaving the pirate raider behind as she steamed toward Yuma.

The crew cheered and Easley waved his hat from the window of the wheelhouse, but Angelina Guiterrez simply stared behind them, clinging to Ki.

"Gone," she said, "Rosa is gone. All your fault, all the fault of the *norteamericanos.* As my father has told me— all crazy, all evil!" She pushed away from Ki and went forward to sit on the deck, arms folded, muttering more of her seemingly limitless supply of Spanish curses.

Gleason was practically dancing with excitement and satisfaction. He jerked Jessie into his arms and hugged her, giving her a deep kiss, which she responded to—but when he let her step back there was no happiness in her eyes.

"What is it, Jessie? What's the matter? We've won, haven't we? Is it Rosa?"

"Rosa, yes," Jessie replied. "That and the fact that we haven't won a thing."

"Not won?" Gleason smiled hesitantly. "But of course we have. Beaten them at their own game."

"We've gotten one shipment through, Ford. One lousy

boatload of goods. We did it through luck and trickery. We haven't done a thing to ensure that the *next* cargo will get through, nothing to keep the pirates from continuing to rule the gulf. We've done our best, Ford, but damn it, it just isn't close to being enough, is it?"

It was a silent boat the rest of the way to Yuma. The crew, elated at first, had found the popular French mate dead in the wheelhouse. Jessie and Ford Gleason stood close together, hardly speaking. The war hadn't been won —only the battle.

Angelina Guiterrez was the most voluble of them all, but her speeches, long, involved, casting about between Spanish and English, were for the most part concerned with which stupid American was responsible for the loss of her cousin.

By the time they reached Yuma at midday and the town turned out to cheer them home, the people aboard the *Grant* acted as if someone had set off fireworks at a funeral.

"What do we do first?" Ki asked a grim Ford Gleason.

"First," the Irish lieutenant said, "we get the quartermaster down here to accept the shipment and have it transported to the post. Then"—he grinned—"we visit Captain Thaddeus York and see if he wants to promote me . . . or court-martial me."

York wasn't half as stony as they had expected. Angelina Guiterrez went stamping into his office, crying loudly about a violation of international treaties, about the *estúpido* American army, the casual way in which the loss of her honored cousin had been accepted by those aboard the *Grant*.

Gleason was expecting the captain to start railing against him, to pull out his hair and finally send in those phony resignation papers. But Thaddeus York did none of those things. Instead he reached into his desk drawer, pulled out a yellow telegraph message, and handed it to Jessie, who read it slowly, then read it again.

79

"From the Ship Registry in San Francisco." Jessie laid the telegram down on her lap. "To the best of their knowledge the frigate could only be a ship formerly called the *Aeneid*, formerly a slaver, taken by the U.S. Navy, refitted, and sold to a California shipping company."

"Thieves, pirates, rapists!" Angelina Guiterrez shouted, standing. "Who are they, who owns this ship? What thieving scoundrels?"

"According to the registry," Jessie said quietly, "a Mexican citizen by the name of Alfredo Guiterrez."

After a long, stunned silence, Angelina grabbed for the telegram, ripping it from Jessie's hand. "Liar," she said with a hiss, but she read the wire and softened her appraisal. "They have made a mistake. There are many ships."

"Maybe," Jessie admitted. "Why don't we find out for certain, Angelina?"

"How?"

"Ask him. Ask your father if he doesn't own that pirate ship."

Angelina Guiterrez was silent, briefly. Again she caused Jessie and Ki to reappraise her when at last she lifted her head and said, "Yes. That is what we must do."

"Anything we can do to help?" Captain York asked.

"I don't see what," Jessie answered. "Have you gotten a reply from San Diego yet?"

"From this Antonio Spinola? Just a message so short our operator barely had time to take it down."

"What was it?" Jessie asked.

"'I'll be there.'"

"That's Spinola."

"What did he mean?" the cavalry captain asked.

"He meant that he'll be here," Jessie said with a smile. The officer shrugged.

"If you were one of my subordinates, I'd grill you, young lady, but so far you're the only one in this hemisphere that's accomplished a thing against these pirates, and if you don't know what you're doing, none of us does.

Will you continue to need Lieutenant Gleason?"

"We will," Jessie said, looking his direction, "most certainly continue to need Lieutenant Gleason."

The army officer looked briefly confused, but he smiled. "Very well, then. The quartermaster has brought in most of our stores off the *President Grant*—all in serviceable condition except for a few crates apparently damaged by shell fire." The captain commented, "It must have been an exciting trip up. I'll expect a full report sooner or later, Lieutenant Gleason. Just now..." he cleared his throat. Just now Lieutenant Gleason was still detached, resigned, nonexistent.

Captain York went on, "If you're returning to Mexico there's one of two ways of doing it. I'm sending a patrol out under Lieutenant Godfrey, Gleason. There's a report of a strike by Heart near Two Wells. You'd be safe with the cavalry patrol, but Godfrey's under orders to look into this Two Wells attack first. That means it would take you a week or so to reach the border at the best."

"A week or two!" Angelina Guiterrez said excitedly.

"Yes." York held up a hand for patience. "The other way is to go back downriver with Easley. He's going to refit in Cordoba—says the locals can't do the job. Ten days from now," York added in a more confidential tone, "there's another shipment due around the Baja Peninsula for Yuma. It's civilian goods, but if you ask me this is even more important cargo than the army materiel you brought through.

"Yuma's dying. I can't be more frank, more clear about it. We've lost half a hundred citizens in the last two months and we'll be losing more. A man can't build a house where he can't come by a hammer or nail. He can't run a shop without goods. He can't eat when there's no food. Yuma's going to return to the Indians if we can't stop those pirates and furnish supplies to our people.

"I'm going to do the best I can," York told them, "to wage war against Heart and Rojas. With the supplies we have now we can proceed far better than before, but those supplies will run out, maybe before we can finish the bandits and the damned Apaches. Stop the pirates, little lady, stop them for this town."

Jessie, who didn't much like being called "little lady," only nodded. It wasn't the time to take umbrage over small slights. It was, as York said, time to stop the pirates.

For once and all.

And if their information from San Francisco was correct, the only place to start was at the Casa Guiterrez. The governor of Sonora had some explaining to do.

"We'll sail with Captain Easley," Jessie said. "Did he give you a time schedule?"

"In the morning, seven o'clock."

"Good. We'll be there. Will you send a courier?"

York nodded. "I'll see that he gets the word." The captain rose. "I've got a commander's call to attend to. Good luck."

And then York was gone, grabbing his hat from the hat tree. In the corner Angelina Guiterrez still sat studying the telegram from the Ship Registry in disbelief. Jessie could almost feel sorry for the pretty, spoiled thing. Almost.

The one she did feel sorry for was Rosa. Come from California to visit her cousin, she had fallen overboard and probably been taken captive by the pirates—seagoing ruthless men who didn't run across a woman for months at a time in all likelihood, and only once in a blue moon did they find a woman as pretty as Rosa floating in the water.

Angelina rose, a little shakily Jessie thought, and walked to Ki. Taking his arm, she walked from the room. Gleason was watching them, one eyebrow raised.

"What now?" Ford asked, and Jessie told him.

"A good eight hours' sleep first of all. We sail in the morning."

"Where do we sleep?" the army officer asked.

"In our own beds for now," Jessie said, but when he came nearer she could feel the heat of his body, his need, and it was very tempting. "For now."

Ki walked Angelina to the visitor's cottage Captain York

had assigned her. She was subdued now, lost in thought. Her right hand was clenched tightly, and Ki knew why. He had seen her take the yellow telegram, fold it, and squeeze it into a tight ball. Maybe this was the first time the woman's eyes had ever been opened to the world, the real world beyond the chandelier-lighted ballrooms and summer lawn parties, milliners, and fawning servants.

"It could all be a mistake," she said, lifting those dark liquid eyes to Ki.

"I said nothing."

"But you think Father is a criminal, the man behind the piracy."

"I think nothing. I am waiting to find out," Ki said gently. They had stopped at the door to the cottage, which was nothing more than a long low cabin chinked with river mud.

"You are a good man, Ki," Angelina said with more feeling than he would have expected. Then she got on tiptoes and kissed him lightly on the mouth. Before Ki could respond she was gone, the door to the cottage closing behind her solidly.

Ki glanced to the hot afternoon sun, squinted through its glare toward the river bed then, nodding to himself, went away whistling to his own bed in the enlisted men's bunkhouse.

He didn't open his eyes, nor as far as he knew even stir until the duty corporal shook him awake at five-thirty the next morning. He dressed, shaved, and staggered out into the early morning to watch a patrol ride out—Lieutenant Godfrey, no doubt, on his way to Two Wells. Then he crossed the parade ground and entered the mess hall to eat.

When he emerged again, Ki was refreshed, ready for the coming day. Angelina, looking pale, wearing no lip rouge, no powder, found him before the building.

"And so this morning I go home," she said.

"Yes."

"And discover whether my father is a criminal," she went on, and a trace of bitterness crept into her voice.

83

"We shall discover," Ki said, "whatever there is to be discovered. You have already considered the worst possibility—anything else can only be better."

She accepted that with a small shrug. When Jessie arrived she looked at Angelina and then at Ki, and he repeated the shrug.

At seven they set off again aboard the *President Grant*, the steamer hardly laboring at all as it drifted down the red, sluggish river. Gleason pointed out the obvious.

"The water's beginning to fall. Look on the side of the bluff there. You can see the old waterline. Another week or so and Easley and his boat will have to stay upriver."

"And Yuma will be cut off again?"

"Unless something remarkable happens," Gleason answered, "like Heart surrendering, and that doesn't seem real probable."

"The next shipment from California will arrive in ten days," Ki remembered.

"Nine now, and those winds that Drew rode down are still blowing, they'll beat that time."

"And our own ship, Jessie?"

"It should be right on the heels of the freighter. Spinola will be able to make better speed, though. I hope."

"I hope so too," Gleason said. "The next time we meet the pirates luck won't be enough."

"Luck and the *California*," Ki reminded him.

"Yes, Drew saved our bacon." Angelina stood away from them as they sailed on past red bluffs and green, clumped willows. Her eyes were forward, on the distant gulf.

"The lady's carrying a load just now," Gleason said.

"She is," Ki agreed. "She—"

The rifle shot from the bluff cut off his words. Ki crouched automatically and tugged Jessie after him. There were a dozen guns, perhaps more on the low bluffs above the Colorado, and they opened up with a vengeance as Easley opened his throttles and steered toward center

84

stream. It wasn't much of a race; the *President Grant* wasn't fleet enough to outrun the bullets of the Winchester repeaters, and the deck of the *Grant* became a scene of bloody carnage.

★
Chapter 9

Ki grabbed Jessie's hand and ran with her to the far side of the wheelhouse, bullets peppering the deck, sending showers of splinters after them as they dove for cover. A sailor had half-pushed, half-tugged Angelina to safety and he had paid with his life for it. A bullet took off the top of his head and, twisting around like a mad puppeteer's marionette, he went over the rail and into the water.

Above them a few sailors with small arms opened up, trying to return the fire of the ambushers on the bluffs. It didn't work. The ambushers had cover and the *Grant* and its crew were easy targets.

A ship's officer crouched beside Gleason, holding a scarf to his bloody face. Ford took the man's binoculars and began scanning the bluffs.

"Indians?"

"I don't think so," Gleason answered without removing the glasses from his eyes.

They were slowly making their escape, but at least three sailors were down, one writhing, moaning pitiably as he tried to drag himself to safety with a broken leg. Bullets pinged off the *Grant*'s stacks and thudded into the woodwork.

"Who in the hell are they?" Jessie asked. "What do they want?"

"I know what they want," Ki answered. She looked at him questioningly. "It's obvious." He ducked as a bullet

86

whipped in close to them and whined off the brass rail behind them. "They have a new plan to stop the supplies from getting through to Yuma. If the steamboats can't make San Felipe, nothing gets upriver."

"The pirates . . ."

"It's not the pirates," Ford Gleason said, finally lowering his glasses, taking a moment to remove the wounded officer's compress and look at the jagged wound, reassuring him some. "I had the glasses on him when he stood up to wave his rifle at us."

"Heart?"

"Rojas. The Águila. It seems our local bandits have their own ideas about the cargoes coming in."

"Such as?" Jessie asked.

"I don't know. But think about this: if no steamboats can reach San Felipe, what happens to the goods? The captains of the sailers are going to unload and leave their cargoes sitting on the docks or in a warehouse. Who gets them then? The pirates?" He lifted his chin to the bluffs, now well behind them. "Or maybe Águila?"

Angelina was kneeling over the body of the sailor with the broken leg. He hadn't made it. The bullet had ripped open an artery and he had bled to death on the deck.

"What is happening?" she asked, lifting dark eyes to them. "Why is everyone killing each other?" Then she stood, blood on her dress and hands, and walked to the rail again to stand there alone.

Easley put the *Grant* in to shore beneath the bluff sheltering the Casa Guiterrez and a small boat took Jessie's party ashore, leaving them on the sandy beach.

Angelina stood for a time looking up at her home, perhaps comparing this homecoming with the one she and Rosa had planned. "Very well," she said at last, "let us do this thing."

They walked up the long winding trail past the same two guards. This time it required no gold bribe to pass through the gates. The Mexicans pulled off their hats and

87

bowed deeply, backing away as Angelina, followed by Jessie, Ki, and Gleason swept through.

The servant on the porch gawked with astonishment, hastily opened the door, and allowed them to enter the house. They found the governor in his office.

"Angelina!" The silver-haired man rose with pleasure and surprise mingled in his expression. Looking at the three people who had returned to his casa with his daughter deepened the puzzlement.

He moved around his desk and stretched out his arms to hug Angelina. Before he reached her she told him bluntly, "Rosa is in the hands of pirates."

"Rosa? What are you talking about? My brother's daughter?" His arms had frozen, outstretched; now they dropped to Alfredo Guiterrez's sides.

"Yes, Rosa, my cousin. I brought her home with me, to surprise you."

"But this is terrible." He looked at Jessie and Ki as if this were their doing. "Something must be done."

"Father," Angelina asked, "where is the *Aeneid?*"

He hesitated just a little too long before he answered, "The what, my daughter?"

His smile had turned into a grimace. Angelina saw as well as the others did that he was lying. She sighed angrily and sat in a chair, looking at her hands, where dried blood still clung.

"The *Aeneid,*" she repeated. "The ship the pirates use. The ship you purchased. The ship that took Rosa from the water."

The governor touched his forehead in an indefinite gesture. He went to his desk and sat in the green-leather chair, and it seemed he was contemplating a lie. He gave it up in exasperation. "Rosa, why did it have to be Rosa?"

"Your daughter was nearly killed this morning," Jessie said quietly.

"Killed?" The governor stiffened. "By..."

"Not by the pirates this time. By Rojas."

"Rojas, the fool . . . !" The governor stopped and then stared blankly at his daughter. He had gone too far to work his way out of his web of lies. He grew defensive instead. "What did it matter if the Yankees lost their supplies? They are in a land they don't own. Arizona is Mexican territory."

"Not any more," Ki pointed out.

"By force of arms," Guiterrez said hotly. "They took it as they took California and New Mexico and Texas. I fought the Americans, fought them at the Alamo. Why? We were reclaiming our own soil. Because some weak sisters in the government were afraid to keep fighting, we lost all of the territory." An arm lifted, indicating distant lost territory. "We have the right to keep the Yankees out of Mexico, we have the right to halt the shipment of arms. Let Heart fight for us, push them out of our land."

"Heart is an ally of yours?" Jessie asked in surprise.

"Heart? No, not that one. He is Apache. An Apache has no allies."

"But Rojas, the one called Águila, is?" Angelina asked. "He is an ally?"

"You cannot understand all of this, Angelina. What do you know of the war? Our family had possessions in New Mexico. All lost to the Yankees. Rojas is a patriot, a son of Mexico. A true guerrilla fighter."

"A butcher," commented Gleason, who had seen things from the other side. The governor seemed not to hear him.

"Your great plan," Jessie said, "has gotten Rosa taken prisoner, nearly gotten your daughter killed, and made a criminal of you."

"A patriot!" A fist banged down on Guiterrez's desk.

"A patriot who could be arrested by his own government. You don't like what happened in the past. All right —a lot of us don't like a lot of things that happened in the past, but they are past, they're fact. Treaties have been signed. What you are doing is illegal and immoral and you know it."

"I!" Guiterrez started to flare up, looked again at his

daughter, and fell silent for a moment. Then he sagged into his chair, looking older, defeated. "I have been doing what I believed was right."

"Right?" Gleason said, and the governor lifted his hooded eyes.

"No Mexicans have been damaged. Only Yankee ships have been attacked."

"Rosa," Angelina said in a tired voice, "has been taken. We must get her back."

"Of course, of course," her father agreed. "But La-Croix . . ."

"Andre LaCroix?" Jessie asked. The governor let his eyes drift to her face.

"You know him?"

"I know he's a cutthroat. He's been hunted from Malaysia to Madagascar. He carries a French name, but his mother was a Pacific Islander."

"Yes, that is the man. He is a useful man," Guiterrez said, his hands making small apologetic gestures, "but sometimes—difficult."

"You don't have any control over him," Ki interpreted.

"He was a useful tool! I care nothing for the cargo of these ships. I only want to strike back at the Americans, to force them out of Mexican territory."

Jessie and Ki looked at each other. Ki had apparently hit it right on the head. Guiterrez had no control at all over his pirate chief. It was enough to pass information to LaCroix, to furnish him with a ship—what he did after that was none of Guiterrez's concern.

"Rosa," Angelina repeated again. She was right, that was the most important point, getting Rosa back from the pirates.

"I . . . can try," her father said.

"You have a way of contacting him?" Jessie asked.

"A note left in a certain cantina in San Felipe. That is all."

"Where is the pirate base? San Tomas Island?"

"I don't know," Guiterrez said helplessly.

"Or on the mainland? A hidden cove?"

"I tell you, I don't know! I didn't want to know. I wanted to keep as much distance as possible between myself and that man, do you understand?"

"So would anyone," Angelina said.

"It keeps the blood from your hands," Gleason said. Ford had seen more of this than anyone and he was bitter. Guiterrez didn't bother to respond.

"Send a note, now," Jessie said, "tell LaCroix just who the woman is."

"Yes, yes, of course," Guiterrez agreed.

"And then," Gleason added, "you can send a message to Rojas. Tell him he's killed enough Americans and if he doesn't stop now his mentor might well find himself dead."

"I don't know how to contact Rojas," was all Guiterrez said. He had lost his will to fight back, to argue. Angelina looked steadily at Gleason, not liking his tone.

"What do we do in the meantime, Jessie?" Ki asked. Guiterrez was scribbling a note. He rang a small brass bell and a servant came into the room, silently departed, and closed the door.

"Find him. Somehow find LaCroix."

"What can you do against him?" Guiterrez asked. "It is madness. Stay here, I will take care of things."

"We'll do what we can to find him," Jessie said. She didn't mention Spinola and his gunship. She could only mentally cross her fingers and hope that the Portuguese captain had good winds behind him.

"I have a boat I can offer you," Guiterrez said.

"All right."

"A boat and crew." He put his face in his hands. "Angelina and I will wait here in hopes of hearing from La-Croix."

"I will not," the Spanish woman insisted.

"What do you mean, Angelina?"

"I mean I won't just sit and wait here while Rosa is being held captive out there. It is our fault, the fault of my own family, and it is a shame that it has happened. It is

91

more of a shame if we don't try to amend what has happened. I will go with Ki and Jessica."

"You will do as I say!" Guiterrez said, the old spark returning briefly.

But Angelina had risen and she looked at her hands as she answered coolly, "No, Father, I do not think I shall do as you tell me this time. Perhaps I will not be able to do that any more at all."

She looked again at her hands and said, "I will wash and change."

Her father watched her go, telling Jessie, "I will see about the boat."

When Guiterrez had lifted himself heavily from his chair and gone out, Gleason said, "I don't really much like the idea of scouting around out there looking for a pirate hideout."

"I don't like it either," Jessie said, "but we have to know where they are. Suppose Spinola does arrive soon— the pirates still have the tactical advantage. They'll know he's arrived and just where he is. They can attack any time they like; we'll only be able to wait. Besides," Jessie said, looking toward the open door, "there's Rosa."

"Yes," Gleason agreed reluctantly, "there's Rosa. Unless the pirates don't get Guiterrez's note in time . . . or care at all who she is."

"Why would they care now?" Ki asked. "They have the ship, they control the gulf. Can Guiterrez call in the federal authorities? I think not, not without getting himself shot. I think LaCroix is going to do just what he wants to do, about Rosa and anything else."

It wasn't a cheerful party that walked to the beach and met the four-man crew of the small sailing vessel Guiterrez had given them. The sea was wide and they were virtually defenseless. For protection, Jessie was counting on the fact that the pirates had no reason to fear what was apparently a small fishing vessel.

The captain of the boat was called Manuel the Small. He was a very big man, vast in fact, with scars across his forehead. What Guiterrez used him for at other times they could only guess, but he was obviously devoted to Angelina, who had appeared in twill trousers, a white blouse, jacket, and dark cap.

"Where do we sail, Señorita?" Manuel asked.

"San Tomas, yes, Jessica?"

"I think we should try it again."

The captain didn't argue or form an expression of any sort. He simply ran up the boat's striped sails, cast off, and caught the current, aiming the vessel's bow south by west.

It was already nearly sundown when they came in sight of San Tomas Island, and the skies were deep crimson and purple when they passed the mouth of the inlet.

"Tonight?" Angelina asked, but Jessie shook her head. She didn't want to sail in there blindly.

"Ask Manuel if he knows another place to beach the boat."

Manuel the Small did, or believed he did. "Once there was an Indian fishing village here. Long abandoned, but there is a rocky beach. Our boat is small, I think we can use it."

In the near-darkness it took another half an hour to round the bleak stony projections of land and find the old village. Manuel put the boat in to the beach expertly, and they went ashore to stand looking up into the highlands, at the stars beyond the bluffs.

Carrying rifles, the crew led the way to the old village, where a few primitive structures still stood.

"In the morning," Jessie said, still looking upland, "we can try climbing that ridge. From there we should be able to see down into the cove. If the *Aeneid* or whatever they call her now is there, it should be easy to spot."

"No fires tonight," Ki warned Manuel the Small.

"No, Señor, no fires tonight."

They withdrew into the trees—twisted, wind-ravaged cedars—and made their beds as best they could. Ki lay awake a long while, apart from the others, covered by a single blanket, listening to the night wind and the splashing of the sea against the rocks below him. Through the branches of the cedars he could see the dully glowing stars, and against the stars a moment later, the figure of a woman.

"I am frightened," Angelina Guiterrez said and Ki lifted the edge of his blanket, letting the woman come naked into his bed.

She slipped in beside Ki and lay still against him for a long moment before her body prompted her to nudge Ki with her pelvis and cling to him.

Ki kissed the woman slowly, mouth, ears, throat, and eyes, feeling her shudder. His hand worked its way across her smooth, milky breasts to her abdomen and lower, resting on her soft thatch, one finger slowly tracing circular patterns against her flesh.

She lay back, her thighs parting slowly, and Ki rolled to her, his hand continuing to work, finding her warmer, damper now as her arms wrapped around his neck and she stretched her neck up to kiss him and then fall away again.

Ki took her hand and guided it to his lengthening, thickening shaft and a tiny gasp escaped from her lips as she encircled it with her fingers, first with a cautious grip and then with a sliding, tugging motion that lifted Ki's need still higher.

He let his head drop to her breasts, took each nipple in turn into his mouth, teasing them with his teeth. Angelina's stroking of his erection became more vigorous as her fingers worked from the root of it to the end, her thumb gently, teasingly running across it there.

She lifted her leg and held it up as she took Ki's shaft and touched it to her inner warmth, taking him in a bare half an inch, her fingers running across his taut sack, along his rod, around her own tender cove, toying briefly with the erect tab of flesh at its head, meeting Ki's own fingers there. Together they worked on the sensitive, tiny erectile organ until Angelina had to lay back gasping, tugging at Ki, demanding that he enter her.

Ki rolled her onto her back, his hands going beneath her

smooth buttocks, lifting her higher as he went to his knees and bucked roughly against her, Angelina's fingers going again to where they were joined, feeling Ki's solid shaft slipping in and out of her, touching her own juices.

She cried out very softly and her hands went to her breasts, her fingers squeezing her taut nipples roughly as Ki, lifting the Spanish woman higher yet, continued to plunge against her, feeling her loosen and grow very damp, feeling her shudder and, with a wild bucking motion, reach a sudden hard climax.

Ki smiled downward, looking into her pleasured starlit eyes. Slowly, without moving at all, he reached his own completion, filling her slowly, copiously until Angelina reached out, fingers wriggling impatiently, and dragged Ki down to her to meet her overheated body, to lie there stroking, gently petting, kissing lightly, earlobes and throat, scalp and lips.

"Are you still frightened?" Ki asked.

"Not so very, not so very," Angelina answered, her voice still breathy, her words shaky. "But the pirates . . . if they come."

And the shout sounded against the night, the bullet cracked through the still air, and Ki knew.

They had come. The pirates were in their camp.

★
Chapter 10

The first pirate Ki saw burst from the trees almost directly in front of him as Angelina dove for cover. The pirate had a gun and he figured he had his man.

That was a big mistake. Ki was already coiled for action, every muscle and nerve fiber in his body alert for instant motion. He moved now as the sailor, tall, dark, bare-chested, held his rifle on the *te* master.

Ki leaped with the quickness of a cat, a flying *tobi-geri* kick nearly lifting the pirate's head from his body as Ki's heel smashed into the pirate's face. Landing, Ki spun, spotting the second raider from the corner of his eyes. Ki snap-kicked the saber from this one's hand and delivered a *nakadata* blow to the pirate's heart. The middle knuckle of Ki's fist seemed to split the man's ribs apart, to strike heart muscle, stunning the raider so that he fell back, eyes rolling, clutching his chest.

Angelina! She was gone, running in panic toward the beach, half-dressed. Ki swallowed a curse and started that way. The crackle of gunfire to his left, farther up the cedar-stippled slope, stopped him in his tracks.

One of those guns was Jessie's .38, the other Ki thought was Gleason's service revolver. The roar of rifle fire threatened to overwhelm the small protesting snaps those handguns made.

On the beach a sailor was clubbed down and killed by three pirates and Manuel, running for the water, trying to swim for safety, was blown to the rocky beach by a bullet that severed his spine and sent the big man sprawling.

Ki had hesitated too long and now he had lost sight of Angelina. He snatched up his vest and started toward the spot where Jessie and Gleason were trying to stand off the pirate horde.

Jessie had emptied her revolver again and her gunbelt loops were low. She crouched behind a fallen cedar, thumbing cartridges into her .38 while Ford Gleason two-handed his Schofield .44, putting a round through the thigh of a charging pirate. All hell had broken loose on the beach below, but it was impossible to tell just what had happened. Cries of pain mingled with savage bellows, crazed laughter. Occasionally a muzzle flash darted flame against the night and yet another man cried out.

Ford had his back to the log, furiously trying to reload now. There was blood leaking down from a scalp wound and his hand seemed to be injured. He dropped half a dozen rounds of ammunition and cursed with frustration.

Jessie was beside him and as a dark form broke free of the night shadows and charged toward them, saber uplifted, she shot the man in the heart. A second shot missed as a pirate attacker dove for the ground and Jessie's bullet rang off the trunk of a massive cedar.

And then the night was still, very still, until a voice from below called out, "All right. I have this woman. Come out now or I will cut her throat. Five seconds only."

The man with the red bandanna over his head did indeed have Angelina Guiterrez and by starlight they could see the knife at her throat. Angelina, half-dressed, hung limply in the pirate's arms, afraid to move, to breathe.

There wasn't much choice. Ford looked at Jessie and cursed again, winging his pistol out into the open area beyond the log. "We're coming out, damn you!"

They had no sooner gotten to their feet than six men appeared to wrap their arms around Jessie and Ford Gleason, shoving them down the slope toward their leader.

They stunk of sweat and oil and the sea. The man who held Jessie let his hand drop and it cupped her breast. With surprise he called out, "Hey, Andre, one more! One more woman."

He stopped, turned her head sharply, and grinned with black teeth. "And what a woman. This sea has been good to us, LaCroix!"

On the beach Andre LaCroix still stood, holding Angelina. He let her go as his men approached and she fell to the ground, panting.

"Any more of them?" the pirate leader asked.

"This is all, I think."

"Yes." LaCroix, who was tall and good-looking in a savage sort of way, walked to Jessie and lifted her head. "The sea is good. Very good."

And he laughed, but there was no humor in it. This was a sea-jackal, a lover of blood, a killer. From the ground Angelina said, "Let us go, you fool. I am Angelina Guiterrez."

"Are you now?" LaCroix asked and he crouched to look into her eyes. "Good, then everything is better and better."

"My father will be angry."

"Let him be," LaCroix answered. His voice was accented in French overtones but carried the nuances of many other tongues, the influence of a hundred ports. "The old fool will pay well for you."

"Let me go!"

"No, my darling," LaCroix, crouching. His left hand went around her throat and slowly tightened. Angelina gasped and tried to struggle free and LaCroix laughed, suddenly pushing her aside.

"She thinks her father is my king!" LaCroix said and one of his men laughed. A bottle of rum had appeared from somewhere and was passed to LaCroix, who drank deeply, wiping his mouth on his wrist afterward. "Your father is not my king, little one. He is only another fool."

"You wouldn't dare harm me," Angelina sparked, sudden fire flushing her face.

"No," the pirate said, "of course not. You are worth too much to me. I think perhaps a million pesos."

"You are going to hold me captive?"

"But of course." LaCroix laughed. "Your father can afford to pay for your return. Until then you shall be hostage."

"My cousin Rosa—is she all right?"

"Your cousin . . .? The woman who fell overboard?" LaCroix asked.

"That's right, yes."

LaCroix stroked his jaw with the back of his hand. "I wish I had known who she was. You see, I gave her to my men."

"You what!"

"I gave her to my men. Amusement is not plentiful out here. I fear . . . she is not of much use as a hostage now."

"You've killed her!"

"No, of course not. But I fear—she has gone just a little mad," the pirate king said.

Angelina didn't answer; she couldn't. LaCroix's attention meanwhile had been taken up by the honey-blonde he was standing before. Long hair curled over her shoulders. Her blouse, half-opened now, revealed marvelous breasts. The pirate moved toward her.

"Stay away from her," Ford Gleason growled, "or I'll kill you with my bare hands."

LaCroix looked at the bloody man before him, smiled, and swung his fist into Gleason's face, dropping him to his knees. "Will you now, will you kill me?" He asked Jessie, "Who are you people, what do you want here?"

"We were visiting with Angelina's father when we heard that her cousin had fallen overboard. We came to help look for her, thinking she might have made it safely to land."

"Visiting Guiterrez? Yankees?"

"That's right. It was strictly business. My brother and I"—she indicated Ford Gleason, who was trying to rise and having little luck at it—"are from Texas. We own one of the biggest ranches there, the biggest, perhaps."

That got LaCroix's attention, as it was meant to. He saw two more potential kidnap victims now and not a woman to be used, a man to be killed as it pleased him.

"What ranch?"

"Starbuck," Jessie answered.

"I have a man who has been to Texas," LaCroix warned her.

"I'm not lying."

"We shall see. Who is alive to pay for you, father, mother?"

"My uncle," Jessie said, just in case this man who had lived in Texas happened to know that Alex Starbuck was dead.

"We shall see then. For now," he said, raising his voice, turning to his men, "leave them all alone. There may be a prize here bigger than any we have taken in the gulf."

Then he ordered the prisoners tied, and they were marched along the beach toward the high-walled cove beyond. Ford staggered, cursed, and apologized, "Sorry, Jessie."

"You did all you could, as I did."

"He's as liable to kill us as not. A rum sot, did you notice that? And a killer."

"He may at that, if we're not lucky," Jessie admitted.

"How can you be cheerful? Don't you realize what a spot we're in? We haven't got a chance in the world, Jessie, not a chance."

"Just one," she answered quietly and, at Ford's curious look, she explained. "Ki, they haven't got Ki yet, and if he's out there, we have a chance."

She looked out toward the sea, not wanting to give her hopes away to her captors, but even if she had been looking to the wooded highlands she never would have seen Ki. No one could have as he glided through the shadows, watching, waiting, knowing he didn't have a chance of beating these odds while at the same time he tried desperately to figure a way.

At the mouth of the cove a longboat waited, and the

prisoners were roughly herded into it to be rowed toward the pirate's hideaway. Ki, on the bluff far above them, jogged after them, finally spotting the four-masted ship at rest in the cove's deep waters, the firefly flicker of lanterns ashore.

He worked his way carefully down the stony bluff. There was a moon rising, but only a thin crescent moon, casting little light through the sea mist. The bluff was very steep, broken, stitched with a tangle of roots.

By the time Ki finally reached the beach on his side of the cove, the prisoners had been taken away, up the far slope to some sort of hidden shelter. Huts, caves, tents— Ki couldn't tell. The firefly lights had gone out, apparently at LaCroix's order, and there was only blue starlight and the feeble, glowing moon.

Ki removed his cotton slippers and started to swim.

The cove waters were warm, but by the time Ki crawled onto the beach opposite he was chilled and fatigued. He lay on the gravel of the beach, watching.

The four-master, swaying gently on still waters. A lone guard walking the beach—but there would be others he did not see. Far upslope, the dim glow of a single lantern.

Ki waited, watching the guard carefully, and when he was at his farthest point, Ki silently sprinted into the trees beyond the beach.

The moon cast soft shadows against the earth as Ki climbed, avoiding anything that looked like a trail. Even so, once he nearly walked into a guard, but the pirate, gun across his lap, was drunk with rum, snoring loudly.

It took Ki fifteen minutes more of climbing, of working his way across the rocks and through the brush of the slope, to find the cave.

That was the pirate's shelter, the dark mouth of a cave, gaping like a baboon's mouth against the hillside. Without the muted light cast by a lantern within it would have been invisible. Inside Ki heard voices, weary, bragging, profane voices. A pirate came to the mouth of the cave, bare-chested, wearing boots and bloused striped pants. He stretched and opened his fly, relieving himself into the darkness, and Ki, lips compressed, crouched and felt the mist.

Were the prisoners inside there? Ki had no way of knowing—if they were, it seemed almost certain that he wasn't going to get them out. The crew of a frigate—how many, thirty men?—and additional gunners or cutthroats. Figure forty. How was he going to take the prisoners from forty armed men?

He backed away down the slope and scouted around a little more, but he found no other caves or shelters of any sort. Apparently, then, he reluctantly admitted to himself, the prisoners were all inside the cave, well guarded.

What, then? Ki's eyes traveled down the slope across the trees and rocks to the dark bay below—and to the sailing ship resting at anchor there.

Ki started back down toward the cove.

He crouched in the brush, waiting for the sentry to turn and walk past him again. Taking care of the pirate was a simple matter. Ki's "Tiger's Claw" attack surrounded the man's vulnerable throat, crushing trachea and blood vessels, and the man was dragged strangling into the brush to die.

Ki rose, looking around in a half-circle. Then he started again toward the ship. There were two armed men at the foot of the Aeneid's gangway. Obviously not the way to go. That meant a return to the water, and Ki slipped from the brush, running in a half-crouch to the dark edge of the lagoon.

He slipped in and swam for a hundred feet underwater to the anchor chain of the frigate. His hands reached up and, tossing his hair from his face, he gripped the cold iron chain.

Shinnying up the chain, he peered over the rail and rolled up and onto the planking of the Aeneid's deck. He waited in the shadows, hearing muted voices, and then, moving silently, he crept along the deck toward the dimly lighted gangway before him.

Ki bellied up to it and peered down. Seeing no one, he slipped into the hatch and slid down the ladder. The sailor at the foot of the ladder was half-asleep, hardly ready for the hard-striking apparition he suddenly met.

Ki thumped his middle knuckle behind the pirate's right ear, paralyzing the cluster of nerves there, and the sailor fell insensible to the deck.

Ki rolled him into the shadows beneath the gangway ladder and moved on, the ship moving gently under him. He found the powder hold a minute later.

The red lettering on the door warned him of the danger of explosives; the iron padlock on the door challenged him to enter. Ki's side-kick removed the door from its hinges and it sagged slowly inward as Ki slipped past it.

He found a candle and matches in a bucket nailed to the wall beside the door, struck a match, and smiled with satisfaction. The pirate vessel had a plentiful supply of all it needed to make war, of powder and fuse and balls. It had all Ki needed to make his own war.

Looking to the door, he let the match go out in his fingers. He rolled a red-painted barrel of powder to the near bulkhead, searched for fuse, and took a guess at its burning time. A yard of fuse was cut from the spool with the edge of a *shuriken* and Ki set it. If it was quicker fuse than he expected he was going to have a problem. If it was much quicker he would have no problems at all; he would be dead.

Ki struck a second match and touched it to the fuse. The deadly little worm sparked to life, writhing toward the powder keg. Ki made for the door, tugged it roughly into position, and sprinted toward the ladder. Behind Ki a man called out and, before he even turned to look, the *te* master had slipped a *shuriken* between his fingers.

Turning, he crouched, the *shuriken* whipping from his hand toward his target. The pirate took the throwing star in the skull and jerked backward, pawing at it. The second pirate appeared at the foot of the ladder, pistol in his hand, question on his face.

Ki took the pistol from his hand with a chop across the wrist, the question from the man's eyes with a two-fingered thrust to the diaphragm. The pirate fell hard, rapping his skull against the steps.

Ki leaped over him and continued on, racing toward the open hatch above him where the starlight gleamed coldly. Ki reached the deck and sprang for the rail, half-expecting a bullet in the back. Diving shallowly, he was swimming rapidly toward shore before any of the pirates on the ship could reach the rail from belowdecks.

Ki reached the beach, started to run, stumbled once in his water-soaked clothing, and ran on again. He wasn't sure how much time he had, only that there wouldn't be enough.

More recklessly than before he climbed the slope, weaving through the cedars, eyes on the cave ahead of him. Some instinct caused Ki to glance behind him at the moment of detonation and he saw the yellow flame flare from the portholes of the pirate frigate, saw her lift at anchor and rock in the water as a cry for help went up.

Ki hit the ground as the pirates stormed from the cavern mouth above him and, with a single exasperated cry, charged down the slope, some carrying buckets.

Ki let them pass and started on. He met a last pirate emerging from the cave, thrust up violently with the heel of his hand, and snapped the man's neck back, smashing his front teeth.

Ki leaped over his fallen adversary and reached the cave mouth, standing to one side, *shuriken* in either hand. He glanced in quickly, saw the two pirate guards, and sidestepped to the entrance of the cave. A throwing star from either hand whistled through the air and the guards fell back, one instantly still, the other thrashing in pain.

Behind him Ki could see flames reflected on the waters of the cove, but he didn't stop to look. Jessie, Ford, and Angelina were bound and gagged, tied in a row on one cave wall next to a collection of barrels and crates.

Ki had them untied in minutes, pulling Jessie to her

feet. "Rosa," Angelina said, and only then did Ki see the crumpled figure in the torn dark dress. He bent to scoop her up and she recoiled violently, a clawlike hand trying to fend Ki off, her black eyes wide with fear.

"Sorry," Ki said and he picked her up anyway, shouldering her as he turned to the others. "Now," he said, "let's go."

"Go?" Angelina said. "Go where? Where can we run to on this island?"

Ki grinned. "There's a slight flaw in most plans." His tone changed. "Move it now. They'll be back."

Ford Gleason looked shaken and bloody, but even as he hobbled from the cave, he had sense enough to crouch and strip the guns from the dead pirates, thrusting the pistol into his belt, giving the repeating rifle to Jessie.

Then they were out of the cave, running diagonally up the hill slope, Ki laboring under Rosa's weight. Behind them they heard more shouts and then, once, what might have been a gunshot, but they were already too far away to even be sure of that.

The moon hovered in a bleak sky above the ridge. That was the only light in the sky as the stars faded into the night mist. Below everything was dark as well. The pirates had gotten the fire out, apparently. Ki had hoped to hole the vessel, but she still sat upright in the water, a thin trail of smoke leaking from somewhere.

"Come on," Ki said, looking deeper into the uplands.

"Ki," Jessie said, touching his arm, "they'll find us. I don't know how long it will take them, but they'll find us if we try to hide."

"What else is there to do?" Ki panted. Rosa moaned faintly and he shifted her weight.

"There's Manuel's boat still. If we could reach it . . ."

"Do you know what you're asking?" Ki said. "To circle the head of the cove on those treacherous bluffs at night, descend the far ridge, and return to the boat on the hope that the pirates, deceived, wouldn't be watching?"

"I know exactly what I'm asking," she said with deter-

105

mination. "I also know we have to get off the island."

"Votes?" Ki asked.

"No votes," Gleason said. "We go. Follow the general."

Gleason didn't look like he could follow the "general" over the next clump of moon-glossed boulders in their path, but he struggled gamely on.

By midnight it was obvious they weren't going to make it, not over that terrain with Ki carrying Rosa, and Gleason injured. Angelina was exhausted and Jessie wasn't doing much better.

They were high on an overlook now. The cove below them gleamed like pewter beneath the fading moon. Far distant they could see a pinpoint of light on the mainland that might have been San Felipe.

Ki had been slogging on over the rough ground, muscles knotted, but he wouldn't have quit on his own until he dropped. When Jessie finally did give the word to halt, though, he wasted no time in placing Rosa gently down and sagging to a seated position himself, drawing deep drafts of cool air into his lungs.

Ford lay down flat on his back, hands on his abdomen. There was blood in his eyes again. His hand had curled up on him. Ki thought it was probably tendon damage.

"Well," Angelina said, "that's it, then. We won't escape."

"We will escape," Jessie said positively. "We just won't reach the boat tonight."

"In the morning LaCroix will send men to watch the boat or sink it—he's a murderer, but he's no fool."

"We'll have to wait and see, then," Jessie said. "For now there's nothing much to do but rest."

Rest and not think about their position—trapped on a small, remote island with no way off, surrounded by cutthroats. Rest and not think about that, not let the idea come to the front of their minds that they would be lucky, very lucky, if any of them lived to see the moon rise tomorrow night.

★
Chapter 11

The sun jabbed at Jessie's eyes through partially opened lids. She rose, rubbing her face, which had attracted a pair of prowling red ants. She rolled her head to one side, seeing Gleason sleeping beside her, and she slowly sat up. Ki was crouched near her feet, watching something intently.

"You see something?" she asked and, without turning his head, he answered.

"They're coming."

Jessie crept up beside him. Below, on the deeply shadowed slopes, she could see a band of men like a long line of insects trailing upward. She counted them quickly. A dozen of them, give or take.

"What now?" she wondered aloud.

"For now, nothing," Ki answered, turning to meet her eyes and then smile. "But something must be done soon."

"Can you see the rest of them?" Jessie asked, brushing back her hair with her fingers, putting her hat on, tightening its drawstring.

"No. They must be at the ship," Ki replied. "They'll want to make her seaworthy as soon as possible. They're out of business without it."

"My plan of getting to the beach, Ki. Is there a chance it will still work?"

Ki nodded. "There's always a chance. It seems certain they'll have people watching there, however. They may have towed the boat into the cove or even sunk it, not wanting to leave evidence of the massacre."

"You wouldn't think they'd care one way or the other."

"They care. Up until now they've had the approval, or at least the tacit support, of the Mexican population. No one cared what happened to the Yankee ships. The pirates may even be some sort of local heroes like Rojas, the bandit. Now they've killed four fishermen. Guiterrez isn't supporting them any more. Slowly LaCroix's little empire may be crumbling."

Jessie realized that eyes were watching them, dark and haunted eyes, and she turned to watch Rosa, sitting up in an animal posture, like some creature withdrawing as far as possible from its keepers.

"Hello, Rosa," Jessie said, keeping her voice soft. "It will be all right, really."

Ki glanced at her. That was a hell of a promise—it would be all right. They didn't look just then to have a chance in hell of getting off the island, even if they could reach the beach; and for Rosa things might never be right again.

Angelina was up now, moving to where her cousin sat. Rosa recoiled even from Angelina's touch, but Angelina put her arm around her anyway and pulled her cousin's head to her shoulder, rocking her.

Gleason woke up very slowly. There was a scab across his forehead. His hand looked bad. Jessie helped him up and showed the soldier where the pirates had been. Just now LaCroix's people had dipped into a ravine, disappearing from sight, but they would reappear—closer yet.

"What I'd give for one fieldpiece," the army lieutenant said. "Blow them off the mountain."

"We haven't got one," Jessie said. "It looks like it's time for a strategic withdrawal."

Ford nodded. "You can't imagine how much of that I've seen in the last six months. Withdraw from Rojas, withdraw from Heart . . . one day, however, I'm going to lead a full-fledged charge. Ki, what are you looking at?"

Ki had been busy scanning the hill slopes, concentration

evident in his dark eyes. He turned and told them, "An offensive weapon, a chance to attack."

"What are you talking about?"

"Look." Ki pointed. "See that jumble of rocks up there? No, not there, just below those three cedars. Rotten-looking stuff, isn't it?"

"What are you thinking of?" Jessie asked.

"Moving the rock," he answered. "Moving it down-slope—very quickly."

"A rockslide?" Gleason asked, squinting that way. "Maybe, maybe—if we can climb that little knob . . ."

"Not we," Ki replied. "You four are going to continue on toward the beach."

"I'm not going to miss out on this," Ford Gleason protested.

"Yes, Ford, you are. You can't climb those rocks, at least not quickly. You're just not in shape for that right now. I can get up there, have my try, and catch up with you again."

"Can it work?" Angelina asked.

"I don't know. At the worst it will slow them down, give them something to think about. It's a chance. The way we're going now we'll have them above us with their rifles when we try to reach the beach. That," Ki pointed out, "would not be a good situation."

"I don't feel good about you trying it alone," Ford said. He reached to his belt. "At least take my pistol."

"No," Ki said, "if the rocks don't do it, a pistol won't do me much good. I think now," he went on, seeing the head of the line of pirates emerge from the ravine, "we ought to quit discussing it and get moving."

"Ki . . ." Angelina was standing beside him now. She said nothing else, she simply kissed him hard on the mouth and went to see about Rosa.

"I'll meet you on the beach, above the Indian huts," Ki said.

"Luck, Ki," Jessie said.

"Yes. Luck." Then he winked and started back up the trail they had traveled the night before, and in minutes he was lost in the rocks and trees.

Ki moved upslope, finding and then losing the men below and ahead of him at intervals. They were small, relentless. From this distance they seemed to be no threat to anyone, but Ki had seen them close up.

He found a wall of crumbling gray stone before him and paused, breathing deeply, looking upward. Then he began to climb, fingers and toes seeking the crevices and outcroppings. The wind had begun to blow off the sea, whisking away the haze, swatting at Ki with menacing fingers.

Once he was up on the pile of crumbling rock he had the time to look below. He thought he glimpsed Jessie and Ford, winding their way toward the beach and whatever awaited them there. He shifted his eyes to the trail below and stood surveying the stacked, crumbling granite boulders around him. He clambered up on them, feeling something give beneath his feet, and he smiled with satisfaction. They would go.

A lever of some sort would have helped, but the only branches Ki could find were from long-dead trees, breaking to powder as he tested them.

He climbed the rocks again, and now he could see the pirates, could make out their faces and the weapons in their hands. He squatted, back to the stack of boulders, and tested them.

He shoved with his powerful legs, feeling something give, but not enough. He looked over his shoulder, saw the pirates crossing the gulley below him, and tried again, straining until his joints popped and the sweat stood out on his forehead. The rocks above him swayed but stayed balanced precariously.

The pirates were nearly out of the gulley now, and Ki swore softly. He had accomplished nothing but to waste time. He tried again.

Taking in soft, slow breaths he gathered his energy,

chanting quietly to himself, seeking his deep inner strength. Then with a great heaving effort he pushed again, tearing his back raw on the stones, and they began to go.

They started slowly, a single flat rock sliding off the hillside, but that rock struck another at the base of the stack, splitting a huge round boulder weathered by the ages in half and bringing the entire tilted column of rock down.

Boulders bounded down the slope, and Ki heard a cry of terror from the pirates below. Each falling rock found another and another and in moments it seemed the mountainside was falling away, thundering down the slope.

Ki went to his belly against a flat, sun-warmed rock and watched. The pirates had nowhere to go. Some tried to run downslope, others to retreat up the trail. The bounding boulders rang down the hillside, sweeping tons of smaller stones and gravel after them.

A huge rock bounced high into the air and crushed one screaming pirate. Others were swept away by the rush of stone. The earth rumbled for long minutes as the stone slid and slowly settled, and when Ki lifted his head again to look through the rock dust he saw only a single pirate alive, and that one was sitting on the slope, holding a crushed leg.

Ki had no pity at all for him, nor for the dead. They had come seeking death and they had found it.

Ki climbed back down the ridge and jogged back through the woods, his eyes on the beach far below.

It was two hours later before he saw the Indian huts, and he slowed, whistling softly, not wanting Jessie or Ford to shoot him by mistake. After a moment a whistle answered his and he went into the camp, finding his friends exhausted but safe.

"The boat," Jessie said. "Gone."

Ki nodded and sagged to the earth to rest, arms around his knees. He had expected nothing else. LaCroix was smart enough to know that only a boat could take his captives from the island. And now there was no boat.

111

Angelina was tired, her face smudged, her clothing torn. She sat beside Ki, took his hand, and leaned her head against his shoulder.

"It's over. We can't get away."

"We will get away," Ki said, not believing it himself.

Ford Gleason looked a little stronger, but still haggard, his injured hand hanging uselessly. "He'll guess that we've come looking for the boat," the army officer said. "And he'll come looking for us."

"We can't go back," Jessie said. "Not up there."

"Then we'll have to fight," Ford said without hope. Fight them all with one revolver, one rifle? Rosa had begun to moan softly.

"They'll take me again," she said, "again. *Madre de Dios,* not again."

"Not again," Angelina said, petting her hair. "Ki won't let them, will you, Ki?"

"No," Ki said, "I won't." He tried a smile, but it was a difficult expression to adopt. He wouldn't let them take Rosa again—just how was he going to prevent it?

Angelina put her fist before her mouth to muffle a shriek of anguish. She was pointing out to sea and now they all came alert, staring that way until their eyes ached.

"They're coming again. The pirates."

It wasn't the frigate, and for a long minute Ki believed it was the longboat with a sail rigged. It was neither. "A fisher," he said. "There's a chance if we can get to the beach."

And an equal chance that if they reached the open beach LaCroix would have them where he wanted them, in the sights of his rifles.

"We've got to try it, Ki," Jessie said, watching the boat slowly sail toward the shore. "Someone's happened along looking for fish."

"No!" It was Angelina who cried out. "Not a fisherman —it is my father. Look!"

And it was. It took Ki a while to focus on the crew of the boat as it glided over the bright, jeweled water, but in

112

the end he saw that Angelina was right. The silver-haired figure in the prow could only be one man. Guiterrez had finally taken a hand.

"We must go to him," Angelina said excitedly.

"Wait for a minute," Ki cautioned.

"This is our only chance!"

"Yes, our only chance!" He took her arm and turned her half toward him. "Still, wait a minute."

The fisher came nearer, the men on board searching the beach. Still Ki held everyone back. But there was no sudden explosion of guns from the shore, no rifles firing from the hills above the beach.

"What do you think, Ki?" Jessie asked.

"I think they are out there, watching," the *te* master responded.

"If they are, we still have to try it," the blonde said.

"I know we do. I just don't like it. I can smell them."

"Now," Angelina said as the boat came yet nearer to the shore. "It must be now, or the boat will be gone."

She was right. Ki didn't like it, but the woman was right, if they didn't try it now the rescue party would sail on, searching the other beaches or the cove itself.

"All right," Ki said. "We will go. Quickly. I will carry Rosa again."

"She can walk, Ki," Angelina said.

"She can walk, but she needs to run. When we leave here we must move swiftly, very swiftly."

"When?" Ford Gleason asked. He was nervous but resolute.

"Now!"

Ford looked to Jessie and began his run, sprinting toward the boat. "Go," Ki said to Jessie and she started out of the sheltering trees as well, a reluctant Angelina on her heels.

The first rifle shots from the hills opened up as Ford reached the beach, waited for Jessie, and ran with her through the surf to the rescue boat. Ki shouldered Rosa and began his own zigzagging run toward the shore.

113

Bullets kicked up sand at his heels and once Rosa groaned as if she might have been hit, but Ki never slowed as he crossed the rocky beach on bare feet, saw guns from the boat answer the firing from the hills, and in hip-deep water delivered Rosa to waiting arms.

Ki slid up and over the gunnels and into the boat as the boat's boom was turned, the sail popping as it filled with wind. Then they were splashing through the light surf, a few stray shots following them toward the open sea.

"Rosa?" Ki asked.

"She is all right," Angelina answered.

"Good, I thought . . ." Ki lifted his head to see Guiterrez standing over him and with him a man in a blood-red shirt.

"I thought you were gone too long," the governor said. He smiled and added, "So I came looking, with my friend—"

"I know too damned well who your bloody friend is," Ford Gleason shouted, and he leaped for the man in the red shirt. In his condition it was no problem for Águila Rojas to club him down with his fist.

"Rojas?" Ki asked, sitting up. He looked back toward the receding shore, seeing only the stick figures of men on the rocks.

"Yes," the man called Águila said with an easy smile. "That is who I am."

He was of medium height, full in the face, hardly handsome, but not bad-looking. He wore an untrimmed black mustache over a narrow slit of a mouth.

"Why, Father?" Angelina asked and Rojas's eyes narrowed with interest as they shuttled to Guiterrez's magnificent daughter. "Why did you bring this cutthroat with you? He—he tried to kill me?"

"An oversight, Señorita," Rojas said, bowing. "Some of my men were overanxious. Too filled with nationalistic fervor."

"Many of your men, it seemed," Ki commented.

"You too were there, Señor?"

"I too was there," Ki answered. Gleason had sat up, Jessie holding his head on her lap. The blonde glowered at Rojas.

"I was there as well, Rojas, and it was no accident that your men were firing at that steamboat. You killed three men in that attack."

"Regrettable. We thought we had found the opposing army."

"The opposing army?"

"Yes," Rojas said with what seemed genuine anger, "the Yankee army, moving into our country again."

"Bullshit." The voice was Ford Gleason's. He was weak and battered, but he wasn't through yet. Rojas started toward him, caught sight of the revolver in his hand and stopped, smiling, hands spread.

"These things happen in war, no?"

"I wasn't aware," Gleason answered, "that there was a war going on between the United States and Mexico."

"Please," Guiterrez said as the voices grew more heated, more tense. "I needed help and Rojas offered it. If he hadn't come to your aid, I am sure you would all be dead. There have been mistakes—many mistakes. Let us get over these mistakes and proceed to do what we must."

"Let us," the land pirate Águila Rojas said, "do what we can to rid these waters of this pirate LaCroix, eh?"

No one answered his words or his deft smile. The island of San Tomas fell away and the boat glided on toward the Rancho Guiterrez.

The governor, appearing worried now, gave each of them a room. Rosa's condition appalled Guiterrez and he sent for the nearest doctor, sitting with hands clasped while the physician examined her.

Rojas spent his time at the sideboard, sampling the governor's brandy. Outside, a dozen of his men surrounded the house. It was difficult to tell if they were meant to be security or wardens.

Gleason had been looked at briefly by the doctor, a

115

sticking plaster applied to his scalp wound, finger splints to his right hand. He had bathed and looked fit and handsome, but he was obviously worried when he spoke to Jessie in her room.

"What does he want, I wonder."

"Maybe he's just being loyal to his boss," Jessie suggested. She wore a pale-pink dressing gown. Sitting before a gilt-encased mirror on a tiny pink-and-white chair, she brushed out her long blonde hair.

"Unlikely to me," Ford said, moving up behind Jessie to let his hands trail down over her shoulders and cup her breasts, naked beneath the silk dressing gown.

"If he sees—that feels good, Ford. My nipples . . . good—if he sees Guiterrez as a future *presidente* or emperor of some new border empire—" Her voice broke off again as she lowered her brush and leaned her head back against Ford's chest. "Perhaps he wants to cast his lot with such a man."

"Maybe." Ford's hands teased Jessie's erect nipples. He bent forward and kissed her neck beneath her soft hair. "It doesn't seem likely, though. I know Rojas. He's a bandit, not a political creature." One hand slipped deeper inside Jessie's robe to cup her smooth, bare breast again. She held it there, turning to smile at the army officer, offering her lips to be kissed.

That business completed, Ford Gleason went on, "He's a bandit and he knows that LaCroix's got plenty of booty. Not hidden treasure exactly, but warehouses full of goods, enough to make a man wealthy. That is what he wants, if you ask me."

Ford lost the thread of conversation entirely as Jessie's supple lips found his again and he sat on her bed, tugging her after him, watching with delight as her dressing gown parted and her magnificent breasts bobbed into full view.

It took Jessie no time to open the housedress all the way and Ford's mind reeled as he let his eyes sweep over her flat abdomen, sleek thighs, the downy patch between her legs. She moved to him, soft and scented, and he kissed

116

her inner thighs, her belly, his hands slipping behind her to grip her solid buttocks and draw her nearer.

"Rojas . . ." Jessie prompted with a laugh, but there was no more Rojas in the world to Ford Gleason as he lay back on the bed and Jessie tumbled after him.

★
Chapter 12

Jessie's lips trailed across Ford's chest, her head going lower. Her breasts nudged his abdomen softly and he reached up to place his hands on her smooth, perfect hips, to let his thumbs dip between her thighs and caress the moist cleft there.

Jessie swung a leg over and was suddenly astraddle Ford, facing away from him. Gleason's hands followed the contours of her shoulders and ran down her flawless back. Jessie lifted herself and took Ford's erect shaft, sliding onto it, bending low to watch as he entered her so that her hair was draped across his legs.

She lifted herself slowly and lowered herself with a wriggling motion. Ford's hands supported her buttocks, reaching beneath her to feel her dampness.

Jessie worked intently at Ford's shaft, swaying and pitching against him. She suddenly sat erect, her head thrown back with pleasure. Ford reached around to tear at her breast with his hand. His loins began to ache with the need for release.

Jessie suddenly lifted one leg and, as gracefully as a ballerina, turned so that she was facing Ford. She sat above him for a moment, head back, breasts jutting, and then leaned down to kiss him, her hair falling in a soft cascade over his head and shoulders.

Jessie lay flat against him then, her hips rising and falling, rotating in concentric circles, her breath coming in soft gasps next to Ford's ear.

Ford reached out suddenly and clenched her thighs, lifting himself, thrusting deeply, hooking his arm around her neck, drawing her face to his as he drove it in deeper, heard Jessie murmur with pleasure, and thrust again, finding a sudden hard release.

Ford's bed remained empty. He spent the night wrapped in Jessie's soft arms, occasionally stirring to run his hand over her breasts in the night, seeing her eyes open to sparkle in the starlight leaking through the window of the Casa Guiterrez.

He slept for what seemed only minutes and when the sun peered through the open window he sat up rapidly, thinking that someone with a lantern was at the window.

"Morning," he muttered.

"Can't be," a sleepy face answered from beside him. "Look again."

"It's morning," Ford said, kissing her shoulder, nipping it lightly.

"Any way of chasing the sun back down?" she asked.

"Afraid not."

"That's what I thought," Jessie yawned. Ford reached for her, kissed her, and she felt his body press against hers, felt his erection begin to nudge her soft belly. "You know what," she had to tell him, "we can't stay here."

"For an hour."

"Afraid not."

"Ten minutes."

She laughed. "What's in it for me?"

"I'll show you."

"Afraid not, Ford. We've got to get back to San Felipe."

"What's San Felipe got but a stinking bunch of fish, rotting wharves, a hotel where assassins try to murder you in your bed?"

"Let's go, come on," she said, pushing him away.

"Thirty seconds?" Ford Gleason asked hopefully, but Jessie was already out of the bed, padding across the bare floor to the washbasin, and all Ford could do was lay back,

119

hands behind his head, and study the perfect body of Jessica Starbuck longingly.

"Hell," he muttered, swinging his feet to the floor. "I ache all over."

"My fault?" Jessie asked, buttoning her blouse.

He smiled. "Some of it." He shook his head and touched the sticking plaster there. He had risen shakily when Jessie said from the window:

"There's an army out there surrounding the house. I wish we knew what Rojas is up to."

"What is any bandit up to?" Ford asked. "Rojas is a little more ambitious than most, though. I wonder if he doesn't really have ideas of building an empire."

"Revolution?"

"Maybe. If so he can use the army materiel that LaCroix has taken from us."

"He knows," Jessie said, turning from the window. She said it with certainty. "He knows that we've got a gunboat coming."

"How could he?"

"Conversation on the army post leaking to civilians? Maybe Angelina blurted something out to her father when we weren't around. I don't know, but that's his game. He wants the ship that Spinola's bringing around."

"Maybe," Ford Gleason said, tugging on his boots. He looked at his injured hand, which gave him some trouble during that operation, and muttered, "Better put the splints back on."

"It's getting complicated, isn't it, Ford?"

"A little. Look, just how does Rojas plan on capturing your ship, assuming that's what he has in mind? From what you told us Spinola will have a salty crew on board, one that knows what a fight is."

"Simple," Jessie said with a taut little smile. "He's got us for hostages. We're as much his prisoners as we were LaCroix's."

"I don't like this a bit," Gleason said, rising to walk to the window himself. Below he could spot three Mexican bandits wearing straw sombreros, carrying rifles. "I don't like it, because I have the damnedest feeling that you're right, Jessie."

"If Rojas is smart enough to work it right he can have all of the coast on his side. LaCroix killed some local men. Rojas, the revolutionary, has arrived to save the citizens of Sonora from the pirates."

"I know it. And once he has those army weapons that LaCroix took, he'll have all he needs to double his present strength, maybe triple it. And our army won't have much at all. I wish I could send Captain York a wire...this is worse than he thought. He was actually cheering up when we saw him last, thinking maybe we had a handle on this. But things just get worse and worse."

"We'll find out soon enough what Rojas's intentions are," Jessie guessed. "We're leaving for San Felipe this morning. Let's see if Rojas lets us go alone."

"I wouldn't make any bets on that," Gleason said. He took the pistol off the dressing table and started to put it behind his belt buckle, but caution caused him to put it under his shirt at his back instead.

"Think that'll do any good?" Jessie asked.

"More than one revolution has been halted with a single bullet," Ford answered, "and I wouldn't have any qualms at all about putting a round into Águila Rojas. I know who he is, what he is. I've seen his work."

Downstairs more bandits milled, some sitting on the marble staircase, others standing together drinking tequila, though the sun had barely risen. They were a hard-looking bunch, most bearded, wearing bandoliers across their chests.

Ford guided Jessie past them and into Guiterrez's den, where they heard voices. It was breakfast time in the casa, but no one seemed to have the stomach for *desayuno* that morning.

Guiterrez was at his desk, his flesh looking gray, his eyes worried. Ki and Angelina were already there, Angelina in a fresh dress of simple design, dark and severe.

"How is Rosa?" Jessie asked first.

"Sleeping. The doctor gave her something."

"Good. Maybe that'll help." Or maybe she was running through endless dreams of endless pirate rapists. "We'd like to borrow some horses, Governor Guiterrez."

"Horses? Of course," Guiterrez said without inflection. He kept his eyes deliberately from the man in the corner, the dark man in the black *vaquero*'s outfit with two pistols, butts forward, around his waist.

"You are traveling somewhere, Señorita?" the bandit king, Águila Rojas, asked softly.

"Yes, that's right."

"Homeward, perhaps?" he asked, his eyes trying to appear amiable, reflecting only evil.

"To San Felipe," Jessie answered.

"A very dangerous place," Rojas said.

"There are others more dangerous."

"Maybe, but I do not feel right about letting a lady ride unescorted to San Felipe, not on these roads in these days."

"She has an escort," Ford Gleason said. The bandit's eyes flickered.

"Two men, not so many. There is the pirate, is there not? A very bad man," Rojas said with a smile that deceived no one.

"We do not need an escort," Angelina Guiterrez said.

"No!" Her father's face flushed and he turned sharply toward his daughter. "You are not going, Angelina. You are home now. Stay here where you are safe."

"I am going," Angelina said.

"What can you hope to accomplish?" her father asked with anguish.

"I don't know," she admitted, "but we have a debt, do we not, Father? A family debt. How often have you told me how important our family honor is? Our family honor is at stake here—we have brought this about. It is our duty to do what we can to make amends for what we have done."

Guiterrez couldn't bring himself to answer. His expression was pained. He looked at Rojas, who was still smiling that false smile.

"Then you see, there is all the more reason for an escort," the bandit said. "Please allow myself and some of my men to ride with you to San Felipe."

"Or," Jessie said, "we do not go."

"That is correct," Rojas said, his smile failing him momentarily. "Or you do not go at all."

"In that case we will accept your offer," Jessie answered. There was no choice in the matter. They had to find Spinola and direct him to the pirate's cove. Maybe Rojas could be taken care of at another time, in another way, but nothing at all was going to be accomplished remaining at the Casa Guiterrez. Jessie looked to Ki, who shrugged almost imperceptibly. He knew. There was no alternative. Rojas had stepped in and made himself a partner in their operation.

"Good," Rojas said. He pushed away from the wall where he had been lounging and walked to the door. "I will see to the preparations. Do not trouble yourselves to bring anything."

"Anything" apparently included weapons. Three bandits entered the room at Rojas's summons and took Jessie's rifle. They searched Ford Gleason carelessly, failing to find the pistol behind his back.

The throwing stars in Ki's vest confused them. Laying them on the desk they called Rojas, showing them to him. He picked one up curiously.

"What are these?" he demanded.

"Rowels. For my spurs," Ki said.

"Poor horse," Rojas said, testing the points with his fingers. "I think you will not need spurs for this ride. Arturo—put these away in my saddlebags." He smiled at Ki. "I do not trust what I do not understand—you, tall man, I do not understand at all."

It might have been nothing but an observation, but it sounded to Ki like a veiled threat. He shrugged. "There is nothing to understand. I am Miss Starbuck's employee."

"Yes." Rojas studied Ki closely, seeing the hard muscle beneath his clothing, the warrior's grace about the man. "And I am only a wandering *vaquero.*"

He had started from the room again before he paused and unexpectedly said, "By the way, Miss Starbuck, when is your warship due to arrive?"

There was no point in denying it. Jessie merely replied, "It depends on the winds."

Rojas said, "Yes," thoughtfully and then instructed his men, "Bring them all along but the governor. Treat them with every courtesy, they are friends of ours." Then Rojas laughed and left the room.

"Cabrón," Guiterrez muttered softly. He realized suddenly that he had been truly beaten, beaten at his own game in his own territory. His head lowered a little and then sank to his desk. Angelina briefly touched his shoulder and then was led from the room, the others following.

Outside the morning was gray. From the south a tropical storm crept toward the gulf. "That will mean heavy winds, will it not?" Rojas asked Jessie.

"Heavy winds, I would think."

"Good winds for sailing, or bad?" The bandit swung aboard his white horse.

"I don't know. You'd have to be at sea to know." They had given her a squat paint pony, at least twelve years old, one carefully selected. It wouldn't run far or fast.

"Yes." Rojas continued to look southward across the gulf. "Do you know what I am doing, Miss Starbuck?" Rojas asked as their party started down toward the coast trail—two bandits in the lead, followed by Ki and Angelina, three more bandits, and then Ford Gleason, Rojas, and Jessie, with two dozen more of Rojas's men following at a distance.

"I think I know," Jessie said, "yes."

But Rojas had the need to talk about himself, to boast, and so he went on. "We are far from Mexico City here, very far. As far," he said with a wave of the hand, "as Yuma from Washington, and our communications, our railroads are not so good as yours. We are very far indeed from the center of power. Some in the capital are worried that we will not long hold Sonora and Baja."

"I understand you," Jessie said. Her horse misstepped and she lifted its head. The sky overhead was clear, to the south murky. The Gulf of California shifted uncomfortably under the influence of the coming tropical storm, the waves building to thud hollowly against the rocky shore and then hiss away.

"Who has power out here, on this frontier so far from Mexico City?" Rojas asked, waving his hand again. "The governors, of course. Their power is nearly absolute—ask our friend Alfredo Guiterrez. No one in the capital knew what he was doing, no one cared. Do you know why? He is a strong man. He keeps things under control."

Rojas stretched his arms in a self-satisfied way, yawning. "It is true in Mexico that the governor has power—it is also true that the man who has power may be appointed governor. You see how that must work?"

"I don't know," Jessie said, growing a little tired of the bandit's speech.

"In Mexico City they must appoint a governor—a friend, a rich landowner, perhaps, who has full control already of the territory, one the peasants dare not challenge. If there is a strong man as governor, they do not have to worry about revolution—do you know *Méjico?* It is a country of many revolutions."

"I know it."

"So you see that what I say is true, *gringa*. Such pretty hair," he added obliquely. "Once a man has power, then what can the officials in the capital do? Send an army of *federales* a thousand miles to uproot him or—what do they say?—legitimize him by appointing the man governor.

"It has happened before, in Durango and in Chihuahua. I know this—I have studied it. The governors of those states are former bandits, respectable now. Soon, little

125

gringa, I shall have power in Sonora, a large well-armed army, and—who knows?—perhaps two gunships! Who then will not say, Rojas, we have appointed you governor of Sonora?"

He laughed then, softly, a self-appreciative laugh that turned Jessie's stomach just a little. He would be governor, he would grow wealthy, and the people of Sonora would pay in the end. Some would die, but most of them would live on as they always had in that dry land, virtual slaves to the powers.

"What do you think?" Rojas asked, touching Jessie's hand. She jerked it away from his grasp.

"I think you are a cunning man," was her answer.

"Cunning? Do I understand that word?" Rojas asked, furrowing his brow. "Clever, *si?"* he asked and, accepting his own translation, he nodded again with satisfaction. "Yes, cunning. You know, *gringa,* if we two worked together, nothing could stand in our way. You could simply order your gunship to do what it has come to do, to destroy LaCroix. You see—order it, do not force me to compel you. Tell the captain that I am your friend. There is vast wealth at stake here, and you and I could share it, Jessica Starbuck. The Spanish, you know, have a weakness for women with light hair."

He tried to touch her hand again and again Jessie's involuntary reaction was to withdraw. Rojas frowned and then laughed. "We shall see, yes? Is it the man with the red hair, Miss Starbuck? Is it the army officer that stands between us?"

"He's only a friend," Jessie said protectively.

"Yes, and I have eyes and ears as well. A good friend, I think." Rojas stroked his chin and the stubble of pepper-and-salt whiskers there. "Think over what I have told you, Miss Starbuck. There are better ways to do things than with violence, no? Better ways than forcing Águila Rojas to kill all of your friends."

The threats were no longer veiled. Rojas had made it very clear. Cooperate or pay the price. There was nothing at all Jessie could do but pretend to go along with the power-crazed bandit as he made a naval war against an equally vicious opponent—winner to control the Gulf of California.

The ride toward San Felipe was silent after that. The storm continued to inch its way northward. It had the look of one of those southern hurricanes that spun and blustered and nearly burned itself out until it became a tropical storm. The winds would still be heavy, and there would be much rain in it.

Jessie watched the storm come and she watched the gulf. Somewhere out there was LaCroix, and somewhere Antonio Spinola was sailing toward her in answer to her wire for help, sailing right into the snare Rojas had placed.

By the time they reached Cordoba it was raining, the wind shifting the horses' manes and tails, gusting against their bodies. The rain was warm, the wind warm, but still Jessie felt a chill.

The steamer *President Grant* was moored at Cordoba, still being refitted after its last encounter with the pirates. Easley couldn't know that it was all probably futile. The chances of his ever taking another cargo north to Yuma were slim indeed at this point, and the people of Yuma, waiting for the supplies that would never come, could only grow angry and disappointed, frustrated, and perhaps violent.

The town would die. Yuma would die and the army would leave southern Arizona.

That left things wide open for men like Rojas and Heart. It wasn't a pretty picture and Jessie rode on despondently, constantly reviewing her failed plans in her mind.

San Felipe appeared out of the rain two hours on. Squat, dark, perched precariously on the beach like a defeated thing ready to surrender to the hammering of the sea, the pounding of the winds.

San Tomas Island was invisible now, but out there an angry LaCroix was refitting his own ship, preparing a war of vengeance. His cannon would be ready, charged, his men

127

worked up to a murderous pitch.

The turbulence the sea was suffering now was nothing compared to the coming violence, the violence of cannon and sabers and rifles. It would come, that too would come. Jessie could feel it as she could feel the wind against her chilled body.

There was death on the wind.

★
Chapter 13

They spent the night under guard at the hotel. The owners of the place stayed out of sight except when summoned and then they were subservient and eager to please. They, too, knew Rojas.

There was no communication between the prisoners. Each was kept locked in his own room, a man outside the door. Below their windows other *bandidos* walked slowly back and forth, cursing the weather.

Ki considered escape. Out the window and into the alley, a quick strike against his guards, and freedom. But freedom to do what? Contact Captain Thaddeus York, who could do nothing to rescue them? Swim out to sea and hope to intercept Spinola? There was nothing to do that made any sense at all and so Ki waited, brooding, using his time to flex his muscles, to practice his movements, keeping body and mind alert for the time that must come—the time when he must kill Rojas or be killed himself.

Finishing his exercises, Ki stretched out on his bed and thought of Angelina, reviewing her milky body inch by inch, remembering what they had shared, each movement and response.

She had changed remarkably. Her world had shattered and fallen away, but she had emerged from catastrophe stronger and more mature. She would endure. If Rojas gave her that chance.

* * *

It was on the third morning, before dawn light had broken through the gray clouds that continued to squat over San Felipe, that a *bandido* came to Ki's door, entered, and said, "Dress, *hombre*."

"What's happening?" Ki wanted to know.

"Dress, *hombre*," the bandit repeated. Maybe he knew no other English, more likely he had been instructed to get Ki and nothing else.

Ki sat up, slipped from the bed, and dressed, the guard's eyes on him all the time, a menacing Winchester in his hands. Downstairs Rojas had gathered his prisoners in the dining room. The windows were dark still, the town quiet. It was early even for a fishing village.

"It is here," Rojas announced. "The gunship."

Ki glanced at Jessie. There was nothing either of them could say or do. Rojas had them and in a little while he would have Spinola's ship as well.

"I think we will advance now to the pier," Rojas said. "You don't mind, do you?"

"Does it matter?" Gleason grumbled.

"I hardly think so." Rojas's cutthroats were around them, all heavily armed. Jessie stood and shrugged, looking at Gleason, who was just mad enough to start something he couldn't finish. She shook her head in silent warning. Rojas approved.

"That is right, Señorita. This is no time for violence. What is gained by such things?"

"Sonora?" Jessie responded and Rojas laughed. The laugh broke off sharply, however, and he turned to his men, giving them rapid orders.

"We will go now. To the pier. Keep each prisoner very close to you. This is it, *hombres,* our moment."

"If there is resistance from the ship's crew?" one of Rojas's lieutenants asked.

"Do what must be done," the bandit leader answered. "I hope, however, that Señorita Starbuck will see that there is no resistance. Why should more people die?"

"I'll do my best," Jessie answered through tight lips.

"Yes, *muy bueno* then, we proceed."

Outside the world was dark, covered by a swirling mist that drifted down from out of stormy skies. The boats along the harbor were dark, indistinct silhouettes. There was almost no one abroad. Those few who were vanished like shadows as they saw Rojas and his men approaching.

At the end of the long pier the sailing ship sat at anchor, lighted only by a lantern at the port rail and another from a foremast boom.

"You will do this properly," Rojas said to Jessie. The warning was implicit.

"I will," Jessie answered. There wasn't anything else to do. A warning would bring an unsuspecting crew into an outlaw ambush. The first to go would be Ford Gleason and Ki.

They stopped at the gangplank, surrounded by lightly falling rain. Rojas's men held Angelina, Ki, and Gleason back out of sight while the bandit leader himself and Jessie hailed the ship.

"Who is it?" came the response to their call.

"Jessica Starbuck. I want to see Captain Spinola."

"He's aboard," the invisible sailor answered with some caution. "I'll rouse him."

It was another minute standing in the dark and rain before the familiar, big-shouldered, ambling figure of Antonio Spinola appeared at the rail.

"Jessica!" he called out. "That you?"

"It's me."

"Come aboard, then. Don't stand in the rain, for God's sake. Come on and have some coffee with old Spinola. Who's that with you?"

"A friend," Jessie said, nearly choking on the word, "just a friend."

"Come on, then—watch the plank, very slippery. Come on and let's hear what this is all about. Pirates?" he asked as they reached the deck and bearlike arms briefly hugged Jessie. "In these waters? Well, in any waters, I guess . . ." Spinola was studying Rojas, seeing or perhaps sensing

131

something about the man. "Come aft to my cabin."

"My men," Rojas said.

"What's that?" Spinola asked, turning back.

"We've brought some other people—fighting men," Jessie said.

"I've got forty men on board, Jessie."

"I couldn't be sure . . . I've brought some more."

"All right." Spinola gave a wary shrug. "Watch! We've people coming aboard now. Let them pass."

"Aye, aye."

Rojas whistled and from the night rain his men emerged, Spinola watching them, measuring them. He glanced at Jessie but couldn't see the warning in her eyes.

"My cabin, then. Come along."

"Ki is here. Also a woman and an army lieutenant. I'd like them to join us."

"Ki! Damn my eyes. There he is. By God, Ki, come along and warm up. You too, young lady," he said to Angelina.

Rojas's people had silently filed aboard and now they spread out along the rails of the ship. Spinola noticed it all, as he noticed everything, but he said nothing. This was Jessie's ship, to use as she saw fit.

In his cabin Spinola turned up his lantern and asked them to be seated. Only Ki and Angelina took him up on it. Rojas stood near the door dripping water on the floor. Jessie went to the far wall to stand near Spinola.

"All right," the captain said, pouring himself a cup of coffee. If no one else wanted it, he did. "What is this?"

"Just about what you suspect," Jessie said with disgust. "I'm sorry."

"This is one of the pirates?" Spinola asked and Rojas answered for himself.

"No, Captain," he said, flashing white teeth, "not one of the pirates—I'm a representative of the government of Sonora. We wish to commandeer your ship to rid us of these stinking pirates."

"Commandeer? You mean steal?" Spinola, who had

seen a lot of seas and a lot of men asked, sipping his coffee.

"Of course not. That is nonsense. We—" From within the ship a muffled sound that might have been a gunshot sounded. Spinola started toward the deck, but Rojas stepped in front of him. "Stay here, Captain, we must discuss this further."

The Portuguese skipper was furious. "If one of my crew has been harmed . . ."

"I am sure no one has been harmed, Captain. It is not our intention to injure your sailing men. We need them as we need you, Captain."

"But if I don't give you my assistance you'll shoot me, is that it?" Spinola demanded.

"Of course not!" The oily smile returned. "We shall simply shoot the hostages you see here. First the soldier, perhaps"—he nodded at Ford Gleason—"and then the tall man, saving the women until you know that we shall do it."

"Damn you!" Spinola growled. He took a menacing stride toward Rojas, dwarfing the bandit leader with his bulk.

"Be careful, Captain. By now the ship is ours. I assure you that the promise I made you concerning the hostages is true."

Spinola looked to Jessie. "What happened, Lady Starbuck?"

"Outmaneuvered, it seems."

"You want to sail after these pirates still?"

Jessie didn't see an alternative. "Yes."

Spinola sighed, banged his empty cup down, and nodded. "I'll need a chart. The weather's bad."

"We have no chart," Rojas said. "I am sure you can find the island we want when it is fully light."

"Through this slop!"

"I believe," Rojas said, "that you have been sailing through this 'slop' for the last week. I have confidence in you, Captain Spinola."

"All right. I'll do it. I suppose by now you've got my crew under guard—I have no choice. A deal? Let these people go and you'll have no trouble from me."

"No," Rojas decided, "I do not like this deal. I will keep the hostages and then I know I will have no trouble from you."

"Does this—*thing*—" Spinola asked, and Rojas winced with fury, "really represent the government of Mexico in some way?"

"No," Jessie answered. "He's a bandit who wants to be king, that's all."

"Silence!" Rojas commanded. They had touched him in a vulnerable spot, it seemed. "This proceeds nowhere. Captain, let us go up onto your bridge. Jessica Starbuck, I think, will go with us. I will have my men escort the others below. By now," he said, smiling, "I am sure they have found several places where people can be confined."

Rojas simply toed open the door and three men entered. One of them had a welt across his nose. Apparently not all of Spinola's people had been asleep or placid.

"Take them," Rojas said. "Leave Miss Starbuck. You have a rain slicker for her, Captain Spinola? I would not want the lady to get wet."

"I've got a spare oilskin, yes." Spinola's voice was taut and whispery with emotion. Jessie understood. Spinola was affable and generous, easygoing as a captain, but he had a terrible temper when he was roused. He was doing his very best to hold it back just now.

Ki led the way to the cabin door, Ford and Angelina behind him. Jessie watched them go, shot Rojas a hard glance, and accepted the oilskin from the captain.

"Why do you look unhappy, Señorita?" Rojas asked. "You have brought this ship to destroy the pirates. Now that is what we will do. Destroy this halfbreed French dog, LaCroix, and make the waters of the gulf safe once more."

Jessie didn't dignify it with an answer. She slipped into the overlong oilskin, tucked her hair in a rubber hat, and waited while Spinola put on his own slicker and cap.

"What's our general course?" the captain asked.

"Almost due east, Antonio."

"Distance?"

"Ten miles, more or less. There aren't any barriers."

"Unless we happen to crease a fisher in this soup. All right, let's get moving. You," he said to Rojas, "get my crew on deck."

"Yes, *Captain,*" Rojas said with a deep mock bow, "as soon as we know which they are."

"What do you mean?"

"Forty men, you said you had aboard. A very large number for sailing even a ship this size, no? I think some of these people are hired soldiers, no? Shall we sort them out ourselves, or will you cooperate?"

"To save time," Spinola grumbled, "I'll cooperate. Line up my men or take me belowdecks. The ship won't sail itself."

Jessie was left with a leering roly-poly bandit to watch her and Spinola was taken below. Ki and Ford had already vanished into a forward hold. Jessie felt as low as she had for a long while. There didn't seem to be a single thing they could do about Rojas.

"I know," she said quietly to a man who wasn't even there, to Alex Starbuck, her father, "you told me there's always a way, but I'll bet even you would have a tough time with this one."

"*Que?*" The bandit cocked his head and leered harder.

"Nothing, nothing at all."

Spinola and Rojas reappeared ten minutes later with a somewhat battered-looking crew. Around the deck Rojas's guards stood watching as the captain gave his orders and the sails of the ship, heavy with rain, were unfurled.

Jessie stood beside Spinola, listening to his shouted foghorn commands, some unintelligible to her unpracticed ears, but carried out sharply by the crew. Behind them stood Rojas, himself in an oilskin slicker now, watching, smiling, looking off into the distance occasionally, perhaps toward some golden dream.

135

In half an hour the heavy sails were filled with the brisk winds the tropical storm had produced, and, groaning and creaking, she swung away from her berth and headed toward the open sea.

"*Bueno, bueno,*" Rojas said. "It is still early. We will catch him sleeping, eh?"

"We can't sail into the cove," Jessie said.

"Why not? He does it."

"I've seen it," Jessie argued, "there's a stone reef across the mouth of it. You have to know the waters well to pass through there."

"Tight cove's no place for a naval battle," Spinola put in.

"We can't sit and wait for him to come out, no? That is no good, it may be days."

"Not days," Jessie said, and she nodded toward the pier they were now passing, where a California packet ship sat moored, waiting to transfer its goods to the *President Grant*. "There's what he's been waiting for. The *Aeneid* will be sailing soon."

Rojas rubbed his hands briskly together. It was the cold that caused him to do it, but it looked like he was overcome by glee. "He will come out," Rojas said, "and we shall have him trapped. A broadside before he knows what has hit him. A 'broadside,' no?"

"That's what it's called," Spinola said. The Portuguese skipper looked as if he'd like nothing better than to turn and wrap his huge hands around the bandit's throat, but that would accomplish nothing at all and he knew it. He bent forward, peering into the mist and rain.

"Bosun!" he bellowed, "send a man aloft. Maybe he can see something from up there. God knows I can't see a thing past the bowsprit."

Jessie settled in then, her back against the cabin, eyes trying to pierce the fog and rain. Somewhere ahead was the island with a waiting armed frigate. There would be a battle and it wouldn't matter much who won. She knew La-Croix and she knew that if Rojas was the winner he would

136

have no further use for them—or maybe he would just have a use for Jessie.

"Spanish men," she repeated, "have always liked women with light hair."

The morning wore on and the sun, half-hidden behind the gray canopy of the clouds, illuminated the sea dully. Still the rain fell, although at moments the clouds cleared and the sunlight fell through them with piercing brightness.

Ki saw none of this. He was locked in a small cabin used for mops and brushes, lye soap and buckets with Ford Gleason and Angelina. Outside a guard was posted.

Ki paced the cabin, if it could be called that, restlessly until Gleason said impatiently, "For God's sake, Ki, knock it off. There's no way out of here, nowhere to go if we got out."

Ki paused and slowly turned. "There may be a moment, however, Ford, when we wish to escape."

"Through solid bulkheads?"

"Through whichever means are available. No, not through the bulkheads, it would have to be the door—or is it called a hatch? You see, it is hinged on the inside."

"That does us a lot of good with an armed man outside," Ford griped.

"We shall see. It is best, I think, to be ready for a chance that may arise than to sit hopelessly."

Gleason had to admit that Ki was right. "You figure it out," he said, "and I'll be with you. Where in hell we could go, how we could get Jessie free is way beyond me."

"It is," Ki said slowly, "beyond me as well, but we will stay ready. Prepare the first step—which is to get ourselves free."

Ki then went to the door, listened, and with a glance back at Ford Gleason showed him something. Ki placed his thumbs on the head of the brass hinge pin and, as if he were opening a champagne bottle, raised the pin.

Ki moved softly away from the door and sat beside Angelina on the floor. "That," he said, "is the first step. Let us sit here and think about what the second might be."

The sky abovedecks was holding clear. Walls of gray mist surrounded them on all sides, but the ship, like a vessel in the eye of a storm, sailed over turquoise waters, the bow slicing a clean path through the sea.

Rojas had removed his oilskin and he stood at the bow rail, holding a shroud line, peering anxiously forward. He nearly leaped with excitement when a soft call came from the mast above.

"Land ho!"

The lookout's cry was clearly heard but the bosun, white-whiskered, red-faced, climbed to where the captain stood and repeated it. "Watch reports landfall ahead, Cap'n."

"All right, Bosun," Spinola said. "Have the gunners make ready their cannon. We've come here for a fight and it looks like it's nearly time for it."

"Aye, aye."

"We'll make a course north by east. If it's San Tomas, we'll circle the island and put into the north of the cove."

Rojas was trembling with excitement when he reached the bridge. "San Tomas, eh? It is San Tomas?"

"It appears to be," Spinola said through tight lips.

"He will come out and we will pounce, eh? How many cannon have you, Captain?"

"Twenty," Spinola told him. "Balls and grapeshot."

Rojas turned to Jessica. "And the *Aeneid?*"

"Sixteen, I think."

"Bueno, bueno." Rojas rubbed his hands together again, and this time the coolness of the day had nothing to do with the gesture. Blood was coming; Rojas was content.

★
Chapter 14

The ship slowly circled the island in a clockwise motion, dropping sail as she came within telescopic sight of the cove entrance.

"Perhaps he is not there," Rojas said with anxiety as Spinola's ship went dead in the water.

"He's there," Jessie said.

"Perhaps we should send out an expedition to make sure."

"And alert him? No."

"Who is in command? Who is making the decisions?"

"You are, Rojas. I just don't want to have to pay for any bad decisions you might make."

Rojas's jaw tightened briefly, then he laughed. He slapped Spinola on the shoulder, a gesture the captain didn't care for at all.

"*Ay*, this is a woman, eh, Captain Spinola? This is a woman."

"Yes."

Rojas caught the censure in the tone of voice and leaned against the rail, staring forward toward the distant cove. Taking Spinola's brassbound telescope from his hand he focused it and shrugged.

"Nothing. Maybe he is gone."

"He'll come out," Jessie repeated. "He's waiting for word the steamboat has docked."

"For word?" Rojas was puzzled.

"Someone will come in a small boat. When we see that

boat arrive, then we'll know that LaCroix will come out after the *President Grant*."

"A boat." Rojas looked with concern toward the mainland. "They might see us."

"Not unless they're looking, and have an eyeglass," the captain said. "No, they won't see us, but from up there"— he lifted his chin toward his topmast— "we'll see them."

Rojas thought that over and then smiled. *"Bueno,"* he said, *"muy bueno.* You are a good captain, eh?"

"Some say so," Spinola acknowledged.

"Maybe when this is over I shall make you an admiral, eh? Give you command of my two ships."

"Your two ships? When this is over," Spinola said, "if all goes well, there won't be anything left of the *Aeneid* but splinters. As for *this* ship, it isn't yours, Rojas. It is *mine*, and it will remain mine unless you kill me." He added thoughtfully, "After which, I will of course be of little use as admiral of your navy."

The ship remained dead in the water throughout the rest of the morning and into the afternoon. The fog came and then went, at times wrapping the ship in damp cottony arms, at other times floating away on the wind to leave the sky and sea dazzling.

It was midafternoon when the word was passed quietly from the crow's nest that a sailing ship had appeared on the horizon.

"Keep your people quiet now," Spinola warned Rojas. "Sound carries a long way over open water."

"Yes. I will tell my men, you tell yours."

"My men," Spinola said stiffly, "are sailors." He turned his telescope southward, watching for the first sign of sail.

It would start soon, Jessie thought. LaCroix would sail out while it was still daylight. He wouldn't try to find that notch in the reef at night. It would start soon and, one way or the other, be ended by nightfall. And she still hadn't an idea in the world how they were going to take care of Rojas and put an end to his mad dream.

"It's nearly enough, Father," she said silently, "to make a person give up."

Belowdecks, Ki wasn't ready to give it up just yet. The ship was motionless, and to him that meant they were off-island, waiting.

"They'll be watching for LaCroix to come out. Unless there's a serious error, he'll never know what hit him."

"That's all very good for Rojas," Ford Gleason said. "I can't see that it does us much good."

"No. The battle itself might, however."

"I don't understand you at all," Ford said.

Angelina sighed. "Riddles, riddles."

"Not riddles," Ki said, crouching before her, hands on her shoulders. "I only mean this—during the battle no one will pay any attention to us. What happens down below will go unobserved when the cannon begin to fire."

"And then you lift the pins from the door and we storm the deck, the three of us," Ford said.

"The twenty of us," Ki answered.

"*Twenty?*" Ford looked at Ki as if he had lost his mind. "What are you talking about?"

"The other prisoners—Spinola's fighting men. They are down here as well, locked in the main hold. Remember?"

"Yes, but . . ."

"Twenty men who were hired because they know how to fight. Men who know this ship. Men eager to strike back, with the element of surprise working for them. We storm the deck during the battle, or at its very end."

"You're an optimistic one, aren't you, Ki?" Ford sighed.

"Yes." Ki grinned. "It is that or die. It causes me to be as optimistic as possible."

"You're right. I'm with you, of course, whatever you decide. But am I wrong, or is the plan a little sketchy? Just how in hell are we going to accomplish all of this?"

"That," Ki replied, "is slightly more difficult, but we will try, Ford, because if we don't, all of us—you, me,

Angelina, and Jessie—will surely die. For now we wait and prepare ourselves as well as possible. Have you still got it?"

Ford nodded. He reached behind his belt and pulled out the revolver he had hidden there.

"Good," Ki said. *"Now,* we may have a use for that."

Out on the gulf waters the fog was settling once again, and the fishing boat had vanished into the cove where La-Croix's frigate lay at anchor.

"He did not see us," Rojas said.

"I don't think so. Likely he would have sheared off if he had," Captain Spinola said.

Rojas's blood was racing. It was obvious that he was enjoying all of this, almost pathologically enjoying it. Perhaps the man had deeper reasons for living as he did than he would have understood himself, a need to have danger around him, blood.

Spinola glanced at Rojas with disgust and accepted a cup of coffee laced with rum from his bosun. "Soon then," he said. "I haven't been in a real sea battle since Madagascar. Pirates then too. Funny, if this is LaCroix, he could have been there that day on the opposite side."

"Was it a good battle, Captain?" Rojas asked eagerly.

"Good? Good battles are in textbooks. This was a bloody mess, is what it was."

"How many dead?" Rojas asked eagerly.

"Seventy men. Three ships sent to the bottom. If we're lucky the bastard LaCroix will strike his colors—assuming he flies any—and surrender before a shot's fired. We've got him pretty well trapped. Once we move to the mouth of the cove he won't have room to maneuver, won't be able to bring his broadsides to bear."

"He must not surrender," Rojas said.

"It would save a lot of lives—those of your men."

"If he surrenders I shall hang them all."

And that, thought Jessie, was exactly why LaCroix wouldn't surrender. "Look."

Her pointing finger lifted toward the fishing boat, now reemerging from the cove.

"That didn't take long," Spinola said.

"They wouldn't have to put in to shore. Maybe they have some kind of signal. Or the sight of the boat itself could be signal enough. That would be safer for the fishing boat crew."

"When do we sail?" Rojas asked. "We must be ready."

"Take it easy, *Governor*," Spinola said. "It takes time to get a four-master into motion." He glanced at his gold watch. "We'll give him at least an hour. Assuming he's coming out right away, he'll have enough time then."

"He'll come out before night," Jessie said. "The reef, remember?"

They looked to the sun, a cold, leaden ball behind the clouds, slowly canting toward the western horizon.

"An hour," Spinola repeated.

It was an hour that passed like a week, a month. Jessie's heart raced and her mouth grew dry. Rojas leaned forward at the rail like a dog waiting to be unleashed. Only Spinola was calm. The giant Portuguese had seen battles at sea before.

Just when Jessie thought that she was beginning to develop little cracks from the tension and that the captain's watch must have long ago stopped, Spinola began calling out orders, and his sailors leaped to the rigging. Minutes later the gunship began to glide softly through the swirling rain over the dull sea toward the dark headland before them.

"Damn it all!" Rojas screamed. He jabbed a finger toward the cove. "I knew it, I knew it! I told you not to delay. Here he comes."

Rojas was right. Through the mist they could see the dark four-masted figure of the *Aeneid* breaching the reef. Spinola simply shrugged.

"He's got a good crew if he got under way that quickly. He knows what he's doing."

"We've let him out, let him out of the trap!"

"He's out of the cove," Spinola said, "but we haven't let him get away. Now, *Governor,* if you'll go down to the deck and see to your men, I'd appreciate it. There's going to be some tricky maneuvering to be done and I'd rather not have your screaming presence on my bridge!"

Rojas just gawked. Spinola hadn't let his temper break through before now, but the sea captain had lost patience with the ranting, bloodthirsty bandit.

"I will go down," Rojas said, and his smile wasn't a pretty thing to see. "Make sure you win this fight, Captain Spinola. You understand me?"

Spinola didn't bother to respond. He bellowed a command to his first mate and summoned his bosun. When Rojas was gone Spinola told the white-whiskered bosun, "No matter which way this turns, Carmody, we're going to have to take care of these bandits when it's done. Pass the word to the crew. If the *Aeneid* goes down, we fight the pirates we have on board."

The bosun looked worried, knowing that the bandits had all of the weapons, but he answered calmly, "Aye, aye, sir. I'll see that the word is passed."

"Gunners at the ready, Bosun," the captain said more loudly. "I'm going across his bow with our starboard side."

There was no doubt that Spinola was going to be able to do just that. The pirate ship had to pick its way through the notch in the rocky reef at quarter-speed. The gunship, under full sail, would cut it off easily.

Aboard the *Aeneid* now Jessie could see tiny, frantic figures rushing across the deck. Faceless things the size of ants—preparing the weapons of death.

The wind seemed to shift and falter and Spinola growled a curse. He shouted something to his first mate, and sailors aloft altered the set of the sails. Below Jessie, Rojas turned and waved a fist, shouting a question she couldn't hear.

Spinola gripped the rail tightly, seeming to urge his ship on by mental force. It wasn't enough. The wind had shifted to the south and was now slowing the gunship. The *Aen-*

eid, meantime, had blossomed with full sail and, as Jessie watched, the *Aeneid* swung hard to starboard herself, placing the two ships on a nearly parallel course. Spinola had lost his advantage.

The gunners below stood ready, looking to Spinola. The range between the two vessels was closing rapidly. Now the men at the rails of the *Aeneid* took on human form. Jessie could see bits of color, bandannas of red and blue on their heads, the glitter of sunlight on bracelets and golden necklaces as the sun broke briefly through, before a following squall nearly erased the pirate ship.

Spinola stood motionless, seemingly imperturbable on the bridge while Rojas, raving, stalked the deck, once stumbling as a gust of wind caused the ship to lurch to starboard.

The *Aeneid* fired first.

Six cannon were touched off at once, balls whistling through the air, all but one falling short as the two ships closed. The single ball that struck Spinola's ship splintered the rail near the bow and rolled across the deck, surprising a bandit who had it slam against his shin, breaking his leg.

"Fire!" It was Rojas who yelled. "Fire, blow them up!"

The bandit leader was going crazy. Jessie saw him slap a gunner on the back hard enough to send him headfirst into his gun. "Fire the cannon!"

Spinola just watched, his head thrust forward, eyes narrow beneath the bill of his cap. Fog briefly swept across the bridge and when it cleared Jessie saw that they were within a hundred feet of the *Aeneid,* where gunners were frantically reloading their cannon.

They still had their ramrods in the cannon muzzles when Spinola nodded to the bosun. The gunners' mate picked up the signal and relayed it along the line.

The gunship's cannon fired in unison, the cannon rolling back along the deck with the force of the recoil until the restraining lines halted their motion.

Rojas cheered crazily as a ball sheared the aft mast of the *Aeneid* and a second struck the forward cabin, passing completely through. Smoke and fire followed the cannon-balls, gusting into the air.

"Grapeshot, numbers three, six, eight," Spinola ordered quietly, and the word was passed again.

The *Aeneid*'s gunners had finished reloading, except for the aft crew, which had been driven to cover by the falling mast. Now the pirate ship's guns answered the roar of Spinola's cannons. Three balls scored a direct hit, but all of them touched Spinola's flank above the waterline, leaving her intact and afloat, able to fight.

"Give her a broadside," Spinola said as if he were at a Sunday picnic, and the starboard cannon were fired simul-taneously, balls aimed at the waterline of the *Aeneid*, grapeshot cutting a deadly swath through rigging and sails and flesh.

Jessie saw pirates blown in half, lifted from their feet and hurled backward; she saw fire, and a desperate group of LaCroix's men rushing to the rail with firearms, to be answered by the guns of Rojas's men along the starboard side of the gunship.

"Grappling hooks," Spinola said. "Reload."

The two warships were drifting ever closer together. Both ships had reloaded their cannon. Rifle fire filled the air, and Jessie could do nothing but duck and watch and await cataclysm.

Belowdecks the tall man turned to Ford Gleason and said, "Now, I think."

Ford Gleason nodded and drew his pistol again. Ki looked to Angelina, motioning her back into a corner of the hold. Then the *te* master returned to the door, doing what few men alive could do—removing the brass pins from the hinges with his thumbs.

Ford started toward the door, but Ki held him back.

"In a minute. You'll know when."

They knew when the ship shuddered, the roar of cannon abovedecks rocking her on her keel, the answering fire from the *Aeneid* thudding against the ship's heavy planking, ripping through her rigging. A boom, or perhaps a mast, thundered to the deck overhead and Ki nodded.

"Now," he said and he gripped the door's edge, ripping it open.

★
Chapter 15

Ki tore the door open and their guard, his eyes on the gangway above where the sounds of battle rumbled, turned with horrified surprise. Ki's foot slammed into the guard's liver and he reeled. A slashing downward chop against the guard's neck put him down for good.

"Now, come on!" Ki called to Ford and Angelina. The ship swayed violently again with the impact of a ball and Ki nearly lost his footing.

It didn't slow him down any as he led the way toward the hold where Spinola's fighting men had been imprisoned. There were two sentries standing before the entranceway to the hold, and though these two were warier than Ki's first opponent, still the leaping *tobi-geri* kick Ki sprang into disabled the first man immediately. Before Ki, landing softly and spinning for a second maneuver, could strike again, Ford Gleason had punched a .44 bullet through the body of the second guard.

Angelina, dazed and more than a little frightened, watched as Ki opened the door and stepped back abruptly. Inside there were men used to trouble and combat. They might have had it in their heads to knock the first man through over the head and try an escape on their own.

"We're in this together," Ki said, and when there was no threatening movement from within he stepped nearer. "It's time to take care of the bandits."

A bull-shouldered man with a black beard stepped forward, hesitated, and then said, "Not Ki?"

"It is I, Nicholson."

"It's all right then, men. I know this one. What do we do, Ki?"

"Find your weapons."

"All right. The armory will be locked, but we can bust it open," Nicholson said. There wasn't time for a further review of their past friendship, of battles they had entered together. Nicholson motioned his men forward and, after a moment's hesitation, they flooded the passageway, racing toward the armory, the best fighting men Spinola had been able to find.

Angelina clung to Ki's arm. He wanted to tell her to stay below, but that could prove more hazardous than going on with him. If the ship took a ball below the waterline it could burst open, flooding violently, and no one left below would have a chance.

He waited until Nicholson had returned, carrying two rifles. "Ki?" he said, offering one to the *te* master.

"I think not."

"Same sort of fighter, huh? Feet and hands. Beats me how you've lived so long. Me, I'll take a rifle or scattergun every time."

The ship lurched violently again and Ki looked to the end of the passageway, where a seam had burst, water rushing along the flooring.

"It is time. Angelina, stay behind the last man, please!"

She could only nod. Her world, made up not long ago of lawn parties and balls, had turned into a violent, bloody maelstrom. Ki looked to Nicholson and Ford Gleason, and started up the gangway to the upper deck.

It looked like the dregs of hell aboveboard. Rigging and booms lay everywhere. Fires burned across the deck. The gunship was alongside the *Aeneid* now and Rojas's men were leaping the distance between the two ships, firing into the bodies of the pirates, who slashed back with sabers or answered gunfire with gunfire.

"Now," Nicholson said. "You know your own mates."

The party of men stormed up out of the hold and onto the deck, Ki looking desperately for Jessie, finding her safe for the moment on the bridge.

Most of Rojas's men were trying to board the *Aeneid* and Nicholson showed them no mercy. His men fired from behind, blowing some of them into the water, others lying sprawled on the deck of the ship.

Screams and cries of pain mingled with the gunfire and crash of falling timber. Ki took Angelina's hand and led her across the burning deck, over snarled lines and broken rigging. A bandit stepped from behind the cabin to confront Ki—one without the guts to board the *Aeneid*, perhaps. He should have done that instead of trying Ki.

Ki snap-kicked him in the groin and as he crumpled up the *te* master gave him an elbow to the face that sent him to the deck. It took only a matter of a few seconds. Ki had barely thought about it. Reflex had summoned the proper blow, and training and skill had directed the blows properly.

Jessie was with the captain on the bridge. Spinola was shouting orders madly, but most of his crew was embroiled in hand-to-hand fighting, and there wasn't much the rest could do with the damaged rigging, with the *Aeneid* tethered to his ship.

Along the rail Nicholson's men continued to fire at the backs of the boarding party and the pirates alike. Anyone on board the *Aeneid* was fair game and the slaughter was terrific.

The fire jutted up unexpectedly. Something flammable aboard the *Aeneid* had caught and was burning furiously. Flames were thrown against the sky as sail and rigging caught. Briefly Jessie saw the captain, LaCroix, saber in hands, bare chest streaked with smoke and blood, and then he was lost in the flames and smoke.

"We'll catch as well, Captain," the bosun said.

Spinola looked to the burning pirate ship and nodded. "Aye. Cut the grappling lines."

The bosun rushed down the gangway to the deck and

with two other sailors began cutting the lines that bound them to the burning pirate ship.

Some of Rojas's men tried to escape from the flames, to leap back toward Spinola's ship, but most were cut down by gunfire, by sabers and billy clubs, and were pushed back to fall into the water or try their luck again aboard the *Aeneid,* where Rojas still fought.

"Cut her free, cut her free!" Spinola was shouting. The men worked furiously at the lines, chopping them until only one was left. This last rope snapped as the ship backed away from the flaming hulk of the *Aeneid.*

On the deck of Spinola's ship there was still a little fighting, but Rojas's men and the few pirates from the Aeneid who had made their way aboard hadn't a chance.

Spinola's ship slowly veered off, only two masts still upright and carrying sail, and she watched the *Aeneid,* a floating torch, vanish in the twisting mist.

They were already out of sight of the pirate vessel when the explosion rocked the gunship to its keel. Jessie was thrown sideways into Ki's arms. Spinola hit the deck hard and rose cursing and shouting:

"The powder hold, damn it all, it's the powder hold."

Already his crew was rushing aft, but the flames pushed them back, and a secondary explosion rocked the vessel.

A bucket brigade began to pass water down toward the smoking hold, but the nearest men could approach no closer than fifteen feet, and it looked like Spinola's ship too was destined to burn and sink into the sea.

The rain started to come down again, in violent squalls, but it did little to halt the flames, which had begun to creep along the deck.

Finally the bucket brigade's efforts seemed to have some effect. The flames died to a crackling roar and then to a steaming hiss. The ship limped on through the fog and rain, and now where there had been a danger of being engulfed in fire, there was more of a danger of being washed away by the rising seas and growing squalls that swept across the deck.

The dead still lay there and they were overboarded at Spinola's command. The bosun awaited further orders. The first mate, gash across his forehead, stood by him, rifle still in hand.

"Course, Captain!"

"North," Spinola said after a minute's reflection.

"North?" The bosun never questioned orders, but this one left him slightly dumbfounded.

"North, I said, yes."

"Why north?" Jessie asked after the bosun had departed to relay the message to the helmsman.

"It's the only course we have. If we strike out for the coast, who knows what we'll find? Rojas may have more men ashore, watching. They wouldn't greet us kindly. South is open water and no chance of refitting"—he looked upward at his damaged rigging—"and we won't make it far without refitting, certainly not to a major port.

"It has to be north."

"To the Colorado?" Gleason asked.

"That's right, to the Colorado. Look at this rain—the river will be running deep. I should be able to navigate it to Yuma with a little luck."

They couldn't fault the captain's logic, but it didn't give Jessie and Ki an easy feeling. They had once seen a sailing ship try the Colorado—the *Aeneid*—and it hadn't had much luck. If they ran aground they would have a long walk across the desert.

"Still," Angelina said, smiling for the first time in days, "we have won. We have beaten LaCroix and Rojas. We have done what we came to do. If we walk, we walk. We have guns and fresh water and food." She walked to Ki, hugged him and stood with her arm around his waist, watching the storm as it broke, curling swells across the bow of their ship, as the rain pounded down.

"She's right, you know," Ki said to Jessie. "Somehow we all escaped in one piece. The *Aeneid* is done for and . . ."

It was then that Ki saw it through the mist. It couldn't

have been, but it was. The *Aeneid*.

"No!" Angelina said in terror.

"Captain!"

Spinola turned slowly and brought his glass up to his eye. "It's the *Aeneid*," he told them quietly.

"She was afire!"

"So were we. The rain, I suppose. But that's what it is. It's LaCroix and he's coming. We must have helped him out," the skipper said grimly, "shooting at Rojas's boarding party."

"Why doesn't he turn back?" Angelina asked. "Why can he be pursuing us? We have no cargo for him to capture! Is the man quite mad?"

"Yes," Ki said. "Didn't you notice that before? Yes, LaCroix is quite mad."

"We've bested him," Spinola said. "He can't swallow that. No pirate could. His crew would elect a new captain. We've bested him and the only way he can save himself from disgrace is to sink us. To sink us and see that every one of us dies."

And, Jessie thought, pirates had ways of dealing out exquisite death. Like burying a man up to his neck on the beach and letting the tide slowly come in and drown him. They had other methods, and LaCroix, who had spent his time on the Seven Seas, undoubtedly knew most of them, methods that made an Apache's tortures look like child's games.

"Closing, Captain," the bosun said, although Spinola knew the *Aeneid* was practically in their wake.

"Yes, yes," Spinola said impatiently.

"We still can beat them, no?" Angelina asked anxiously. "We still have more men, and we still have more cannon. Many cannon."

"Young lady," Spinola had to explain. "That explosion aft was our powder hold. We have the powder in our guns and maybe another load after that. When that's burned we have nothing at all."

"He can't know that!"

153

"He doesn't need to know it. He's coming after us and that's that—look at *that*, the gall of the bastard!"

The Jolly Roger had been run up from the topmast of the *Aeneid*. A leering skull with crossed bones beneath it, skeletal hands holding a glass of rum, casting dice. La-Croix had run up his true colors at last.

The rain continued to fall in heavy sheets, the wind gusting across the deck of the ship as it leaned into the wind, plunging downward, then rising slowly, creaking and groaning. In the rigging the wind shrieked like a banshee horse. The ship seemed held together by little more than luck and a few seamen's prayers. The fire had long ago gone out, but the deck was charred and broken away. Spinola bent his head into the wind, looking for the mouth of the Colorado. The *Aeneid* seemed nearly to kiss their aft rail with its bowsprit. Twice Spinola ordered the stern cannon, swivel mounted, small gauge, fired into the A*eneid*'s wheelhouse, but that accomplished nothing at all. LaCroix had a fever in his heart and he was going to keep on coming until they somehow stopped that heart.

It was nightfall before Spinola's sailing skills put some distance between himself and the pursuing pirate vessel. With nightfall the sky seemed to sigh and clear, sunset purpling the world, the clouds drifting away over the desert, and suddenly they saw the dark notch that was the mouth of the Colorado.

"It's luck now," Spinola said. "Neither of us has any right trying to sail that damned river. Upcurrent, at night. There'll be bars and snags."

"And so?" Jessie said.

"And so, we'll try it and we'll beat the rascal, too. Sailed the Congo once with a privateer in my wake. Only one of us came back out of that damnable river."

And it was Spinola who had lived to tell the story. He had no fear of the river ahead of him, the river that now would be frothing, racing southward against their bows. He only had a fear of losing to the pirate behind them.

The sea pushed them forward and the river countered

that force with its own current. The sails were set again, Spinola tacking one way and then the other, trying to catch the feeble wind, to bull his way up the raging Colorado.

Behind them Jessie saw no light, no sail against the sky, heard nothing, but she knew LaCroix was there. The river bluffs began to rise, deep red in daylight, black now. This was the stretch of water where Rojas had ambushed the steamer, trying to keep it from reaching San Felipe. Ironically Captain Easley was now free to take his *President Grant* into port, accept his cargo from the packet ship, and steam northward without fear of pirates.

And Jessie wished they were aboard the *Grant*, paddling steadily upriver, without fear of wind or current or sandbars.

"There he is," Spinola said in a low voice. No one else saw the pirate vessel by the time they turned and looked through the night toward where the captain was pointing, but they had no cause to doubt him, none at all.

They sailed on upriver in a laboring back-and-forth motion, Spinola using all his skill to keep the deep-hulled ship sailing on. The Colorado fought them all the way. The white water frothed and moved around them, as powerful as sea surf, bringing with it trees and snags and sediment. Boulders the size of small houses rolled past, occasionally banging off the hull of their ship, carried on by the powerful current of the angry, rain-fed river.

It took most of three hours to make the next mile. The shore was dark and empty, a wilderness indifferent to their struggles. The crescent moon, dully glowing, rose after midnight, lending a little visibility, but only a little. It seemed to magnify the peril of their situation as it gleamed on the racing waters of the Colorado.

Spinola pushed on. They were all exhausted. Jessie had taken to watching a landmark on the eastern shore, a huge, malformed knob of rock that looked like a horse's head turned sideways. For nearly an hour she watched it as the ship tacked toward one shore and then the other, laboring but seeming to gain nothing.

155

The bosun had returned, drawn and weary, eyes pouched. "Captain, we're taking on quite a bit of water now. Sprung some planks back there."

Ki had seen the beginning of that and for a long while he had been wondering why the damage hadn't been worse. Now, apparently, it was getting worse, a lot worse.

"Pumps broken out?" Spinola asked calmly.

"Yes, sir. Men have been working steady on it for most of three hours."

"You didn't report it before."

"Sir, you didn't need a report like this and there was nothing you could do but order out the pumps. Mate did that. Now you need to know. I've reported."

For a moment Jessie thought the captain was going to explode in the face of what could have been called insubordination; instead he astonished her by hugging the bosun to him with one arm.

"All right, Carmody. You've reported. Keep the men at it." And at that moment Jessie knew why Spinola was a respected captain.

Rounding a bend, they saw the Colorado widen, felt the current slow as the bluffs fell away to flat, sandy desert. The width of the river here slowed the rampaging current and for the first time, as the sails filled with fresh wind and the ship noticeably picked up speed, she thought to herself, "We're going to make it."

A minute later they ran bow-on across the sandbar.

★
Chapter 16

The ship plowed into the unseen barrier. The bow dipped and the stern lifted from the water, throwing them all forward roughly. The gunship shuddered as if it would have liked to come apart there and end it all, but it stayed together.

It stayed together, but it was firmly hung on the sandbar. Spinola had his men in the rigging in moments, shifting the sails, but the wind had all but died, and what little breeze there was seemed to be blowing head-on against them.

"Damn all, damn all," Spinola said. "Drop a line, give me the fathoms," he shouted.

"What are you thinking, captain?" Ki asked.

"I did it in the Congo, I'll do it here. If a man can stand down there, Ki, we'll tow it off by main force. If not we'll try the longboats. If we have to, we'll run lines to the shore and back her off that way. We'll get around the bar, assuming there's a way," he added dryly.

"Assuming," Jessie said, "there's time."

They turned slowly, knowing what they would see. The frigate was a quarter of a mile downstream and coming on with demonic implacability.

"Damn all, and us turned wrongside. Pilot! Fathoms!"

"One fathom to port, half to starboard, ten to the stern," a voice from the darkness called back. He didn't have to report the bow depth. The bowsprit of the ship was jabbing upward toward the starlit sky.

157

And the pirates were closing yet.

"Into the water on the starboard side. Bosun! Rig lines to the stern. Drop those boats, damn all! Boats away!"

Ki glanced at Ford Gleason and the army officer gave him a look of silent agreement. They were doing no good there. They peeled off their shirts and Gleason shed his boots, then it was over the starboard rail with the sailors into the rapid-running waters of the Colorado River. If the gulf waters had been warm, these were stunningly cold, and Ki gasped as he went in waist-deep, the current threatening to knock him from the sandbar.

Stern lines were rigged and heaved to the sailors. Spinola's idea was to tow the stern of the ship upstream and drift off the bar. His secondary thought was that he could bring his cannon to bear if he were sideways in the river.

If they could move the damned thing at all. Longboats splashed into the water, eight men rowing each boat.

When both longboats had been rowed toward the eastern shore and their lines were taut, the men along the sandbar began to heave.

Ki heard the joints of his shoulders pop, felt the muscles along his back and thighs stretch, grow taut, and surrender. The big sailing vessel wasn't going to budge.

"Heave ho!" Someone began to shout a cadence to them and the sailors worked to it. On the "ho," Ki and Gleason gave it all they had. There were no slackers on that bar. They moved the ship or they died. They pulled until their heads ached and muscles seemed to bleed beneath their skin. Still the ship remained fixed.

Still the *Aeneid* closed and now, as the crew watched in alarm, LaCroix began to set a different course, to wheel her over until she was broadside to the floundering gunship.

"Heave ho!" came the call again and there was futility in the cry. The waters swirling around Ki's hips were icy, swift, debilitating. He strained again, strained until cold sweat broke out on his forehead. He could see Gleason,

158

eyes closed with concentration, shoulder muscles standing out like twisted rope.

The moon was in Ki's eyes. He could see the dark desert beyond, the stars gleaming brightly, the long line of sailors tugging against the ponderous weight of the ship. He could see the *Aeneid* closing, a madman at its helm, and he knew they hadn't a chance in hell.

"Heave ho!" They pulled again and a rush of unexpected current ran over the sandbar, knocking half a dozen men to their knees, to rise choking and gasping for air. And at that moment the ship came free, the stern backing around into the current. Spinola yelled, the men still aboard the ship cheered.

"Get back on board!" someone shouted, but already the men were running, swimming, leaping for the ship. The guns of the *Aeneid* opened up before Ki reached the rope ladder. A half-dozen tongues of fire, a boom like distant thunder, and cannonballs struck wood, others splashing into the water, sending up thirty-foot spouts of water.

Ki reached for the ladder. It swung away as lead impacted with oak and he went down briefly into the icy water. Rising, he felt a hand grip his wrist and saw Ford Gleason above him, clinging to the ladder with his injured hand, anguish on his face. Ki clambered up.

Sailors hit the deck in a mad dash toward their positions. Ki saw Spinola, hands behind his back, watching the *Aeneid* as if she were nothing more than a curious sea creature. Then he nodded and the cannon of the gunship roared with their own war-thunder. The deck rolled under Ki's feet. He could see the soft arcing course of the cannonballs as they were lofted through the air, and he could see the deadly devastation they wrought as five of the portside cannon scored direct hits.

A mast toppled on the *Aeneid*. Spinola turned and said something Ki didn't get, but a sailor beside him repeated it. "That last one was below the waterline. She's dead now!"

"Reload, be quick about it," the gunners' mate was shouting, his voice loud but oddly calm. Spinola's men had all seen combat before. "Powder monkey! There's a can left there. Take it to number one, smartly!"

The guns roared again in unison and the *Aeneid* failed to answer. Ki, nearing the bridge now, saw the effect of these shots himself. Two below the waterline, where already a gaping hole had been ripped in the pirate ship, the third ripping through the foremast's moorings, toppling it like a big tree.

Aboard the pirate ship men were diving for the water. Along the rail someone ran, shooting into the water at the fleeing sailors. LaCroix.

The next cannonball ended that. It struck nearly on top of the pirate chief and Ki saw him blown away to the far side of the ship.

"Grapeshot, Captain?" the gunners' mate called. Spinola nodded, and the next battery was more fiercely destructive than any that had gone before as grape was loaded and sent hurtling through the space between the two vessels. Anyone left alive on the deck of the *Aeneid* would have been ripped to pieces by the deadly barrage.

The guns fell silent, but the night was still alive with primitive sound. Wood burning hotly, a ship sighing as it canted and slowly sank, the cries of wounded men, the river raging past. It lasted for most of an hour and then there was nothing. The *Aeneid* sank until there were only two masts visible, and then the current of the Colorado carried her away, bumping and scraping downriver toward the gulf and her final resting place.

The silence then was amazing. The river continued to hiss and froth against the flanks of the sailing ship, but on board no one spoke or even seemed to breathe.

"Over?" It was Angelina who broke the profound silence with her question, hopeful and nearly childish.

"It seems so," Ki answered.

"Some of them must have made it to shore," Gleason said.

"They won't come back unless they're fools."

"Over," Angelina repeated with wonder. "Rojas—La-Croix."

It was over, but how long would it be before it was truly over for those like Rosa, or even the crusty but now twisted Ansel Barnes, the Yuma sutler who had set out with cannon on his steamboat to try to defeat the pirates? How long would it be before Guiterrez felt that it was over? How long before the rift between Angelina and her father could be healed?

Ki stood there with his arm around Angelina as if he were supporting her, but the truth was he needed someone to lean on himself just then. It had been a long battle, and the type of battle he was not used to—the sea had its own rules for survival.

"Course, Captain?"

"North, of course. Find a way around that bar."

"Yes, sir. Fell right through it," the drenched sailor answered with a grin.

"Then you know the course, Pilot," Spinola answered. "Powder gone?" he asked.

"Near gone, Cap'n."

"Ball gone?"

"Near gone, Cap'n."

"Rum gone?"

"Not half, sir."

"Then break it out, sailor! Double ration—but not an ounce more. I mean to sleep tonight, and you know how the second starts to howling when he has more than a few."

"Aye, aye."

The gunship started on again, but the Colorado was still too shallow for her, and a mile upstream she ran aground again. Spinola's crew, rum mugs in hand, stood looking up expectantly at their skipper. They were smoke-smudged, bloody, some half-drowned, and they had done a legion's work that day. They waited and waited.

"Drop anchor," Spinola growled at last. "Hell, a man can only do so much."

The *Aeneid* was sunk, the pirates dead or dispersed, Rojas presumably dead. They sat at anchor in the middle of a wild storm-swollen river. There was no point in pushing on. As Spinola said:

"I need my sleep. The rest of you do what you want. Yuma tomorrow one way or the other, and then out of this damned country for me and these open-sea men."

The sky was starry, the thin moon oddly bright, silver and sharp against the sky, the dark circle of it showing clearly. The Colorado rushed on, but it couldn't threaten the battered sailing ship, which lay at rest, silent and dark at midstream.

"I'm sleeping too," Jessie said. Gleason nodded. He looked to need rest more than any of them. The soldier had taken a lot the last few days. His smile was bright but weary.

"Me too."

"Ki?" Jessie asked and he answered:

"After a while. Perhaps I feel the need to enjoy this moment. The stillness, the calm."

Jessie nodded and staggered toward the deck. She glanced back once and saw that it wasn't the stillness Ki needed to enjoy at all. He had Angelina Guiterrez in his arms and her head was tilted back to meet his kiss.

The river was cold, but the night air off the desert warm. Ki stroked Angelina's hair and smiled at her in the night.

"Frightened again?"

"No, not frightened," she answered. "I just want you to make love to me. All of this"—she gestured toward the empty land, at the vanished turmoil of combat—"it is inside me still. Tension, a need to scream or fight."

"I know," Ki said.

"You have felt this way before?"

"Many times, after a battle. A need to find myself alive, to prove that death has not yet touched me."

"Yes," she said thoughtfully, "something like that, I think." Angelina watched the waters flow past for a time.

162

"I need to get off this ship, Ki. I feel as if I have lived on ships half of my life."

"All right. We can take a longboat to shore."

"Yes," she said eagerly, "just to walk on land. To find a place to lie down where the world is not shifting under your feet. I would like that."

Under the eye of one of Spinola's guards Ki helped Angelina down into the longboat and with powerful strokes he pulled them to the shore, beaching the boat.

It was still, only crickets and, upriver somewhere, grumping frogs breaking the silence of the night. They walked then, arms around each other's waists while the thin silver moon dipped low and the stars brightened.

They found a sheltered beach where the sand was dry and warm and there they made their bed, Ki stripping his clothes off first, Angelina adding hers to make a sleeping place.

Ki stood before the woman, running his hands along her sleek thighs, over the contours of her hips, across the gentle mounds of her breasts, and Angelina smiled in the night.

She kissed him deeply, her lips parted, and reached down to find his shaft and caress it, bringing it to full life. Angelina lay down then on her stomach and Ki went to her, kissing her shoulder blades, the small of her back, her thighs, and she shuddered, her legs slowly parting, her hips rising.

Ki moved in behind her as she rose to her knees, her head cradled on her arms. The crickets continued their chorus. The night wind was warm, somehow stimulating. Ki found her cleft and touched his rod to it, slowly entering her moist depths as Angelina quivered eagerly, reaching back to touch Ki, cradling his sack in her palm, touching it to her.

Ki rested his hands on her sleek, full buttocks and slowly swayed against her, taking his time, deeply enjoying each sensation, each point of contact.

Angelina began to thrust against him, to rock and pitch,

to make little contented sounds deep in her throat. Her eyes were half-shut, unfocused, her mouth open so that starlight gleamed on her teeth. Her hair was fanned out against the bedding. A patch of sand showed on one arm. Her fingers, outstretched, cut grooves in the sand beside her with each stroke Ki took as he spread her and drove it deeper, now practically lifting her knees from the ground with each thrust.

She gasped again and Ki saw her eyes close tightly as she lost herself in sensual joy. He bent low and kissed her spine, reaching beneath her to cup one breast, to torment the taut dark nipple there.

Then slowly he straightened again, his hand trailing down her spine, and as she began to work at him with her inner muscles, to urge him on, he felt the need rising in his loins build to a frenzy.

He buried himself in her, his head thrown back, all of his concentration focused on the point of contact, on the deep rhythmic strokes, until the sudden flood of his climax rushed forth.

He stayed there, hands caressing her buttocks, body trembling, the wind warm and soft across his body, until the tenseness was gone, until he wanted nothing more than to collapse against her. Then he withdrew and lay beside her, hands prolonging her glow as he rubbed her shoulders, traced patterns on her back, followed the line of her spine from her neck to its base, gently touching nerve endings, sending a tingling warmth flooding through Angelina's body.

She scooted closer to him then and clung to him. The night was warm, the battle was over. There was nothing to fear in all the world. Her man slept with her.

Dawn was clear, a flourish of colors briefly painting the now-distant clouds crimson and gold, deep purple and orange, before the desert sun, white-hard, dominating, climbed into the pale sky.

Ki and Angelina had been back on board the ship for

two hours by dawn, but there was no point in trying to go to sleep. They stood at the rail in silence, watching the stars shift, the eastern horizon go gray, the river flow past.

Jessie, yawning, joined them just at dawn. She had a cup of coffee in her hand and told Ki and Angelina, "There's more below. Gallons of the stuff."

Angelina shook her head. "I guess not," Ki said. Captain Spinola, stretching, peering upriver, came on deck. He stood looking at the hole in his deck, at his battered rigging, and then shrugged.

The captain walked to the rail where the three passengers stood and leaned beside them.

"I suppose," he began, but that was as far as he got. A bullet from the shore punched a bloody, ragged hole in his arm and Spinola was sent thrashing to the deck. Simultaneously the war cries sounded from the sand dunes and Heart's Apache raiders charged forward, firing repeating rifles at the ship as the crew dove for cover or raced for their own weapons.

"Cannon, cannon," Spinola roared from flat on his back. Ki was crouched beside him, ripping open the captain's jacket, trying to get a look at the bullet wound, which had already smeared the deck beneath Spinola with blood.

"Bosun!" Spinola shouted, angry with himself for being injured. "Where in hell are you?"

"Here, sir." The white-bearded bosun ran toward them in a crouch as the handful of armed sailors at the rail tried to answer the attack of the Apaches, who had nearly reached the beach now.

"Bosun . . ." Spinola couldn't finish giving his order. There was no one to give it to. An Apache bullet thudded into the bosun's face and exploded out the back of his skull.

"Hold still," Ki ordered. "You'll bleed to death."

"Ki, get the gunners' mate. Any of the gunners . . . use the cannon."

"All right, yes." Ki nodded to Jessie, who took over

165

with the wound as Ki sprinted across the deck, drawing rifle fire himself, searching for a gunner.

He found one man he recognized as a gunner crouched in a hatchway, and he shouted at him, "Captain says to fire the cannon. Any of them primed and loaded?"

The man just stared at him with bleak eyes. He had had enough over the past few days. Ki repeated the question, yanking the sailor to his feet.

"Are they primed and loaded? Which ones?"

"Numbers two, three, and six. Ball loads."

"All right. Where's your punk?"

The gunner finally had gotten hold of himself. He straightened and shook away from Ki. "I'll fire the guns. It's my job, sir. Powder monkey! Bring me a punk."

The powder monkey, a dark kid of twelve or thirteen, pale and shaken but determined, delivered a burning punk to the gunner. He never got a chance to touch off the cannon with it. He winked at Ki and then fell over dead as a bullet bored its way through his spine and blew him forward into the hold.

Ki picked up the burning punk and crossed the deck to the cannon. There was no time to figure how to aim them. He simply touched the powder hole of number two and got out of the way as it roared its deadly message and rolled back on wooden wheels before the lanyards brought it up.

Ki peered shoreward, watching his ball explode behind a half-dozen rifle-carrying Apaches. A fountain of sand blew skyward as the ball hit the beach and one Indian was flung cartwheeling through the air.

The others retreated toward the dunes and seagrass, and by the time Ki fired his second cannon they had all but vanished, leaving four dead behind: three on the beach, one floating facedown in the water.

The ship's gunners had been assembled finally and they took up their positions. Ki handed his burning punk to one of them, but he only shrugged.

"Won't do me any good, sir."

"What do you mean?"

"This." The sailor kicked over a red can of powder and it rang hollowly, trickling a few grains of black powder before it rolled away down the sloping deck of the ship. "The powder hold, sir, remember. What we had in these guns was all there was. Maybe Smitty there's got a reload. If he does he's the only one."

The gunner's mate had finally made his appearance. He had a good excuse for being slow in arriving. He was dragging a heavily bandaged leg behind him.

"Load half-charges," the mate ordered. "We don't need range here."

"How many loads will that give us?" Ki asked.

The mate tried to smile. "In the neighborhood of four, I would say, sir."

The Apaches had begun sniping from the dunes and Ki turned at the cry of pain as another sailor went down. He touched the gunners' mate on the shoulder and worked his way forward, a bullet tearing splinters out of a cabin wall within inches of his head.

Jessie had Spinola's coat off, had him bandaged as well as possible. Ford Gleason had appeared in his undershirt and he fired from the rail with his handgun, once grunting with satisfaction.

"Think I got that one," he said.

"That only leaves us the problem of what to do with the other fifty," Jessie said.

She looked to Ki and he shook his head. "The gunners' mate says no more than four loads."

"Damn all." Spinola continued to writhe and curse. He tried to get up but Jessie wouldn't let him get any farther than to a sitting position. "Small arms issued?"

"Yes, Captain," Ki said, realizing he was talking to a man who was already halfway to being delirious with loss of blood.

"Give her a broadside," Spinola said and then his head sagged back heavily.

"We couldn't be in a worse position," Gleason said. "Stuck in the middle of the river."

"They can't know we're almost out of powder. They've got to respect the cannon."

"Maybe. If Heart's tenacious enough, he'll discover in the end that our cannon no longer work."

"Here they come again!" someone called and the sailors did their best to hold back the charging Apaches with small-arms fire. One of the cannon was touched off prematurely, and it fired its ball well in front of the Indians.

"Hold your fire!" Gleason yelled, but they weren't his soldiers. No one at all seemed to be in charge. A second gunner fired his cannon and, cursing, Ki returned to the gunners' mate.

"Save those last charges until they really count."

"Just now, sir, they all seem to count," the mate answered, but he ordered his gunners to hold off anyway.

The Apache weapons fire was too fierce for Ki to risk returning to the bridge, and so he ducked beside the rail, watching the fight. Another sailor was shot and fell over the rail into the river, to float away as Apache snipers continued to fire at his body.

A long ululating war cry brought Ki's head up and he saw a dozen of Heart's men, dressed in white, red headbands around their long dark hair, sprinting toward the beach.

"Will they really count now, sir?" the gunners' mate asked with dark irony.

"Yes," Ki replied softly. "I think so."

The cannon belched flame and smoke and rocked back, the balls, guided by more expert hands and eyes than Ki's, doing a lot of damage, one impacting in the center of the Apache charge, the other sailing just behind them, striking two Indians who were fleeing the first ball.

Then the Apaches were gone, the beach still but for the shifting smoke of the cannon.

"Well, then," the gunners' mate said to his men. "Small arms for us, boys."

The mate shrugged at Ki as if to say that's all we can do. Ki scowled with frustration and, still in a crouch, returned to the bridge, where Angelina watched him with dark, frightened eyes.

"That's it for the cannon?" Ford Gleason asked.

"Afraid so."

"Maybe he'll back off," Gleason said without believing it. He had seen Heart fight before. The Apache leader's war was a holy war. He wanted to drive the whites from his land. He wouldn't quit coming.

And if he didn't . . . Gleason looked at his own handful of spare ammunition and then down along the deck where half a dozen sailors lay dead.

"Here they come again," someone called and Gleason crouched, two-handing his revolver, waiting for it to fall uselessly on an empty chamber.

★
Chapter 17

Heart's warriors advanced more cautiously this time, but whatever their source of ammunition, they didn't stint when it came to burning it up. Their new Winchester repeaters punctured the flanks of the ship with .44-40 slugs, inevitably touching flesh now and then, cutting down the defenders' numbers.

"The cannon," Ki said.

Jessie looked at him. Ki was right. The cannon should have been fired by now, would have been if there had been any powder to feed them. Heart was no fool. He knew now. He knew he had the whites.

Still the sailors fought back stubbornly, and Heart's braves advanced only slowly, no more than two warriors reaching the water's edge.

These two did more damage than the others combined. They crouched, performed some action Ki didn't understand just then, and rose again with bows and arrows. The arrows were coated with burning pitch. They lofted through the air to strike the sails high above, and the canvas burst into flame.

"Get that down, get that down!" Spinola ordered hoarsely through his pain-inspired fever. His eyes were glassy, distant, but he was still involved in the battle—or perhaps he thought he was on the Congo River years ago, fighting pirates.

"Cut the sails, damn you, you monkeys! They'll gut us."

Three sailors immediately leaped for the masts. Two of them were shot down by Apache rifles before they could do anything at all. The third man climbed into the rigging, knife in his teeth, sawing at the shroud lines through the smoke and flames until a huge sheet of floating canvas smothered him with fire and he fell screaming to the deck.

"Burning," Spinola muttered. "Bucket brigades."

There was in fact already a bucket brigade at work, but they couldn't do much to halt the spread of the flames, and soon the sails were gone, the masts scorched brands standing against the pale Arizona sky.

"Belay that!" the second mate shouted at the bucket brigade. "Get to the rails. We haven't gained much if we save the cabins and the Apaches get to use them."

Nicholson, who had been fighting from the stern rail for nearly an hour, made his way to the bridge. He glanced at the captain and then at Ki.

"Who the hell do I report to? We've got something like twenty rounds apiece, and—" He ducked as a bullet cut near his head, turned, and, cursing angrily, fired at an Apache attacker. "Nineteen rounds," Nicholson said, managing a grin as he crouched again.

"We're not going to be able to hold out," Jessie said.

"No, miss, not for long."

"Until dark?" Ki asked.

"Dark? What the hell does darkness do for us? They can swim to the ship, board her, and eat us alive."

"I was thinking," Ki said, "that we would not be here after dark."

"Go through them?" Nicholson asked incredulously.

"No. The far shore. If we can reach it we have the advantage. They would have to cross the river and take us from our position."

"I don't like it," Nicholson said.

"No one likes it," Gleason said, "but I think Ki's right. We're in a nearly indefensible position." Gleason glanced upward as a bullet struck the cabin wall above them.

171

"What do we do after we reach shore?" Nicholson wanted to know. "Lie and bake in the sun? Walk fifty miles to Yuma?"

"We will do," Ki answered, "what we can. It gives us a chance."

"A damn slim chance."

"Yes," Ki agreed, "a damn slim chance."

"I'll tell the men to pick their shots carefully. If Heart doesn't mount a full assault we should be able to hold out until nightfall."

Gleason said, "There's no need for him to risk his men in a full assault. He's got us, he knows it."

"Perhaps," Angelina said, "we could go down the river again. In those little boats."

"There's too many of us, miss," Nicholson told her. "Besides, we'd have less chance that way. Apaches would follow us along the bluffs and pick us off. There's no shelter in a small boat like that."

"Perhaps help will arrive," Angelina said hopefully. "From up the river."

"Heart will know that first, too. You can bet he's got lookouts up on the bluffs, watching for something like that."

Jessie could see the despair growing in Angelina's dark eyes. She said unconvincingly, "Perhaps help will come, but in the meantime we're going to have to do what we can to help ourselves."

"Here they come again," a man shouted. His shout was cut off short, however, as a bullet ripped through his throat. Ford Gleason turned grimly and started firing, while Nicholson made for his men aft.

Jessie just looked at Ki. They had been in all sorts of unimaginable situations where only a miracle could have pulled them through. Maybe they had used up their supply of miracles. Maybe this was the last battle for Jessica Starbuck and Ki.

The Apaches came on again and the air was filled with the thunder of the guns, with drifting powder smoke, and the cries of the wounded and dying.

The battle lasted throughout the day, with Heart probing their weakness, charging at intervals, at other times sitting back to let his men snipe away. By now he knew several things. The ship was going nowhere, for one thing, despite the heavy current of the river. For another, the cannon aboard the ship were useless. And by now his probing must have convinced him that the whites were low on ammunition, very low. They fired only when they had a clear, close target, and the Apaches offered few of those.

"Just until nightfall," Ki said under his breath. If they could only hold out that long.

"Here they come again!"

The sun hung overhead for what seemed an eternity, scorching exposed flesh, blinding red and weary eyes, eyes bleary and unfocused from the constant watching. Now and then a round was expended on nothing more than a bush moving in the wind; now and then a call went up that the Apaches were coming when nothing at all moved on the beach.

Night came, but it came so slowly, the glow of sunset fading so softly, that when it had settled it seemed a dream, some impossibility their constant wishing had produced.

The world was silent. The wind blew, shifting sand. The river muttered past. The frogs were silent on this night. Men walked among them, Apaches, deadly and silent.

"Now," Ki said, "before the moon rises, before Heart comes again. Now!"

They filed toward the port rail, anxious eyes gleaming in the starlight. The longboats were tugged into position on their lines. Two boats. Each of them would have to make two trips to the far shore.

The current hadn't abated. Rowing back to the gunship would take some doing. "Over the side," Ki said to Angelina.

"I'll wait and go with you."

"No, you won't. You'll go now, and so will you, Jessie."

173

Jessie smiled in the darkness. It wasn't usual for Ki to order her to do anything. He knew she had a mind of her own, a will of her own. He must have been very worried indeed.

"All right," she agreed, only because someone had to go first, and who was to say it was any safer ashore than on the ship? No one had mentioned it, but they all knew there was a possibility that Heart had men on both shores.

Spinola, half out of his mind, was lowered in a hastily improvised sling. He was the last one in and then the long-boat glided away, rowed by the ship's crew.

Nicholson refused to leave the ship in the second boat, as did Ford Gleason. They helped to lower the wounded into the longboat, and once, as they discovered after they had lowered a man, the dead.

The corpse just lay there, grinning up at the stars, and one of Nicholson's hardened fighting men choked with disgust and kicked the body overboard, making a too-loud splash.

The boats returned silently half an hour later. It was just within five minutes of being too late. Ki slipped down the rope ladder and into the boat when he felt Gleason touch his shoulder. Around the curved bow they could see silver against the water where the surface of the Colorado had been disturbed by something.

Ki jabbed an urgent finger shoreward and the boat pulled away, even as the Indians were silently climbing the rope ladders on the other side of the ship.

The boat glided away on the current and moments later they saw the flames billowing skyward aboard the ship, saw briefly a band of madly dancing Indians silhouetted against the flames. They had the white ship; they had destroyed it. Heart's magic was good.

"Bastards," Nicholson muttered and he raised his rifle, but Ki put a hand on the barrel of his gun, lowering it.

"It isn't worth it. Save the ammunition for when it counts."

The boat fought the plunging, furious current for most

of fifteen minutes. When they finally managed to beach it they were a good hundred yards from where the other survivors had taken shelter in the dunes.

"It's us," Ki called out softly as they neared the position. He didn't want to get shot by his own people now.

"Ki?" Angelina came out of the darkness of the river shore to hug him. "We saw the flames."

"Everyone is off."

Everyone that was going to get off.

Ki bellied up to the top of a sand dune to lie beside Jessie and Ford Gleason, Angelina beside him, gripping his arm tightly. They lay there and watched the flames lick at the deck of the ship, consume it, and slowly turn it to charred wood and ash that drifted away on the current, its last remaining mast slowly toppling, vanishing into the dark waters, the clinging flames dying.

"Another good ship gone," Spinola said. "Damn them all, another good ship gone to the bottom."

They watched until there was nothing left to see. The Apaches, content with the destruction they had caused, didn't try to cross the river, not then. The moon was rising and they would have made very good targets.

"We could try to walk out now," Nicholson said.

"In the darkness? We'd be lucky if we didn't walk into a nest of Apaches."

"They'll have us come daylight—if he's the general I think he is."

Ki didn't respond to that. No one did. Nicholson was absolutely right. The Apaches would have them come morning, no matter what they did.

Only Ford Gleason knew the area well and he had been trying to get his bearings, staring at the landmarks the rising moon brought to life.

"I haven't been this far south much," he told them, "but there may be a way. There's supposed to be a high trail, up along the bluffs. If it comes to a fight at least we'd have high ground."

Ki turned and looked to the bluffs, a hundred feet high,

black and mysterious above the river. "Can we climb those?"

"That's the question, isn't it?" the army officer said. "Some of us probably can. Others—" He looked at Spinola, who was raving about Madagascar.

"A runner, Ki?" Jessie suggested. "Someone to try for Fort Yuma and return with the army while the rest of us hold out?"

"Two days, Jessie. At the very minimum."

"No man is going to run through those Apaches and the desert heat," Gleason said. "We all go together or we sit here and fight it out."

"And die here?" Nicholson said. "My vote's for trying the bluffs."

"It will kill the captain and half of the others," Angelina said.

"Young lady, staying here isn't going to ensure them of a long life either. Let's get the healthy ones out—if we can."

If they could. If Heart didn't come again. If the burning heat of the desert day didn't kill all of them one by one. They still needed that miracle, Jessie thought. It didn't show much promise of arriving in time to do any of them any good.

★
Chapter 18

The Apaches came at first light, trying to cross the river on horseback, their war cries sending chills up the necks of the survivors on the far shore. "Pick your targets carefully," Ford Gleason reminded them quietly. "Let them get a little closer."

Since reaching the shore Gleason had taken command and no one objected. This was his territory, these his old adversaries.

Heart sent half a dozen warriors to their right flank, the horses fighting the current as the Apaches fired from horseback. To the left, nearly out of rifle range, a dozen more Indians forded the river. Gleason was more concerned with these than with those downstream. These could cut off their planned path of retreat. Did Heart have their tactics figured out? It seemed likely. There was no survival for the whites unless they reached Yuma.

The rifles began to fire, puffs of smoke rising from the dunes. One Apache had his horse roll on him at midstream, and he floated away toward the gulf. All but one of the others reached the shore and vanished into the dunes.

"This is no good," Ki said, and he was right.

"He's already got us flanked."

"I know it," Gleason said grimly. "And likely more than we saw have crossed over."

He turned to look toward the rising red bluffs. The sun peering over the horizon shadowed them deeply in the gulleys and highlighted the promontories with golden light.

"Feel up to it, Jessie?"

"The climb? If we have to. What about the wounded?"

"They go," Ford said, "or stay and let Heart close his trap around them."

They slipped back from the dunes then one by one, and started toward the distant bluffs in a loose file. The injured, carried or supported by their comrades, staggered along or begged to be left behind.

Spinola was one of those. "Leave me, you blithering idiots! Don't let 'em cut your throats for an old salt's sake."

Ford Gleason halted and said once clearly, "Shut up, please, Captain Spinola. We're not at sea now and I'm in charge. I'm ordering you to be quiet and you'll be quiet."

Spinola smiled thinly. His face was pale and drawn as Ki and the gunners' mate carried him forward, down through a sagebrush-clotted gulley, and up the sandy slope opposite.

Only once did Spinola say anything else. He opened one eye, saw the gleaming white sun, the white sands and chaparral, and muttered, "Hell of a place for a sailing man to end his days."

Reaching the bluff took half the morning, but that was the easy part of it. Gleason, panting, perspiring freely, stood at the base of the cliff looking upward. Then with the nearest thing to despair Jessie had yet seen in the man he looked hopelessly to his ragtag army.

"It's a bitch," he muttered, "purely a bitch."

"It's the only way?" Jessie asked.

"The only way I know of. We can't stay along the river bottom, that's for sure."

"Where are they?" Nicholson wanted to know. "Where are the goddamned Apaches? Why haven't they hit us?"

"Do they need to?" Ford Gleason asked. "The bluff will do it for them."

"We'll make dandy targets up there," the gunners' mate panted. No one needed to hear that.

"Onward and upward?" Jessie asked, brightly she hoped.

"Upward at least."

"Damned hot," Spinola muttered out of his delirium, "no rum rations today. Bosun—no rum, not in this heat."

"Ki?" Ford asked. "Do you see a way up there?"

"No good way. We can only try it. Up that gulley." Ki pointed. "Along the little ledge. It looks narrow, but maybe..."

Maybe was all they had. Jessie's miracle hadn't materialized. They began to climb, hauling the wounded with them. The gulley Ki had indicated was littered with rock and rubble. For each step forward they seemed to fall back two. The sun was a blazing brand against their necks, turning the rock beneath their hands to a searing stovetop.

And below were the Apache snipers.

Each moment Ki expected the guns to open up, for all of them to be blown from the rocks by the Indian sharpshooters, but Heart's guns held back. Somehow they reached the trail a hundred feet above the beach, and they collapsed to pant for air, to hold their sides and shield their eyes, peering toward the glitter of dunes and river below.

"Something's wrong," Gleason kept saying. "He should have hit us while we climbed. Something's wrong."

"Maybe he didn't need to waste the ammunition," Nicholson said pessimistically.

"What are you talking about?" Ford, nerves frayed, demanded.

"Maybe, Lieutenant, he didn't need to try sniping us off the rocks because he's waiting for us ahead. Just sitting, waiting for us to walk into his arms."

Their eyes went up along the bluff trail to its red, barren terminus. Nicholson shrugged apologetically.

"It doesn't matter now," Ki said. "There's no other way to go but up."

"No." Gleason looked back down the bluffs. Far away he could see a few charred timbers, all that remained of the gunship resting on a sandbar across the Colorado River. "There's no way to go now but up."

He rose heavily, tugging Jessie to her feet, and they started on beneath the white sun. Ki had given over Spinola to one of his men and, touching Jessie on the shoulder, he moved up beside Ford Gleason.

"I want to go on ahead, Ford."

"Why?"

"To scout the trail out."

"All right," Gleason said after a moment. "Take a rifle."

"No," Ki said, "you know me better than that, Ford. I am carrying my weapons."

"They won't do you much good against an Apache gun, Ki. But," the officer said, sighing, "you'll do it your own way, I guess."

"It is the way that has served me in the past."

"Yeah." Gleason's wounds were still nagging him. The sun and exhaustion had beaten him down. He was as determined as ever, but his resources were fewer.

"Ki," the lieutenant said, "thanks. You and Jessie— how could anyone have done more? It's just too bad things had to work out this way."

"It isn't over yet, Ford. Not yet." Ki smiled a smile he didn't feel and then he went on ahead, trotting softly over the rocks on the broken trail, his bare feet silent and swift.

Ahead, above, there would be Apaches if Heart was not a fool, and he struck none of them as that. A sentry posted here and there, ready to light a signal fire if the escaping whites appeared near his position, or perhaps a mirrored signal winking across the river. Then the weary band of survivors could simply be circled and, one by one, eliminated.

The sentries, if this conjecture was accurate, had to be eliminated if they were to survive. They would have to be eliminated quickly and silently—and that was Ki's specialty.

He glanced behind him. The straggling party of men and women was out of view now, lost beyond a bend in the trail. Above, Ki could see the rim of the bluff, a scattering of pale-green, bristly vegetation. Nopal cactus and mesquite.

And then quite suddenly he saw the white-shirted Apache warrior.

Ki paused and crouched, pressing himself into the shadows cast by the red bluff, knowing that it was motion the hunter's eyes saw first. By remaining still he confused the eye, by being as one who is not there, by letting even his own mind believe that he was not there—for there were moments when thought passed from mind to mind in ways quite inexplicable but quite real.

Ki concentrated on other lands, on Japan, on wide emerald seas, and when he glanced up again, the Apache, his long hair drifting in the wind that gusted up the face of the bluff, had turned his back to walk slowly way.

Ki moved then. He darted up the trail, bare feet avoiding each stone and twig. Reaching the head of the trail, he crouched, peering upward through the cactus.

Two Apaches crouched, facing each other, speaking in low voices. They could have been brothers. Flat-faced, dressed in white, red headbands, two studded Winchester rifles.

Ki slowed his breath and focused his concentration. He would have no second chance. He tried to foresee each movement he would make, to anticipate each countermovement the Apache sentries might try.

There was no more time. The first sailor had appeared around the bend in the trail. Soon the Apaches would rise and return to the rim of the bluff. It had to be now.

Ki was up and over the rim like a vengeful wraith. Everything seemed to be happening too slowly. No matter how he urged his body on it was too slow, too slow.

He saw the Apaches' heads turn, saw recognition in their eyes, saw them start to rise.

Ki launched himself through the air, body all angles and power. His *tobi-geri* kick snapped back the head of the Apache on his left and sent the man, neck broken, to the

181

sand. The man to his right tried to swing his rifle around but Ki kicked it from his hands.

The Apache rolled to one side and came up in a crouch, knife in his hand, the blade turned upward for a disemboweling slash. There was no fear and little surprise in the Apache's eyes. He was a warrior and he had fought long.

Still he was puzzled by this barefooted apparition, and as he feinted and tried to rip Ki's abdomen open with his knife the sudden effectiveness of Ki's downward block, a *gedan-barai,* startled the Indian. His knife was there, gleaming in his hand, driving upward toward Ki's exposed belly, and then it simply stopped, motion frozen by the *te* master's movement.

The Apache jerked free and tried again. Ki's crossed wrists again halted the driving thrust, catching the Apache's arm just above his hand, carrying the motion on through as Ki's viselike grip closed around the Indian's wrist. The knife arm of the Apache was raised high and Ki's knee drove upward into his groin. The Indian sagged, still struggling, and Ki finished him with a sharp chop to the base of the neck.

The Apache fell to the ground and lay still against the Arizona sand.

Ki squatted on his heels and waited, slowing his heartbeat, surveying the land around and below him. Had it done any good at all to take the lives of these two men, or was Heart still very much aware of where they were?

It was another fifteen minutes before the entire party, sweating, legs trembling, some of them bleeding profusely, made it to the rim.

There was still no time to rest.

"Yuma," Ford Gleason said, pointing northward. There it lay, tiny at that distance, dark and squat. Ford's chest rose and fell heavily. "We've got to keep moving."

He looked at the two dead Apaches, nodded respectfully to Ki, and started his battered party forward along the rim.

The wind was very dry despite the nearness of the Colorado, which showed below as a darkly gleaming ribbon winding through the red canyon. They staggered rather than walked, their eyes on Yuma, that incredibly distant, shabby mecca. It seemed to grow no nearer no matter how they hurried.

"Stay out of the jungle," Spinola cried out. "Stick to the water, men. Crocodiles be damned!"

Jessie looked at Ki, exhaustion evident in her face, and Ki could say nothing, do nothing to cheer her. Angelina fell and lay still. Ki returned and yanked her to her feet. It was no time to slow.

Behind them the long line of Apaches had appeared along the trail. Healthy men, armed men, men used to running through the heat of the desert day.

There was no way, no way at all they were going to escape this time. Gleason ran like a man in a dream. His head bobbed. Some elusive thought kept circling his mind, like a great bird refusing to perch.

It came with the first crack of a pursuing Apache's rifle. "Two Wells," he gasped and Ki turned to look at the officer, not understanding. "Two Wells—that way. The little settlement."

Ki understood then, and they slowed slightly. Down the interior hills a small town stood, nearly lost in shadow. Red hills folded around it. It was nothing much at all to look at, nothing you could imagine as a refuge.

"This way!" Ki called and the others, stunned, simply stared as they halted raggedly. Leave the trail, bolt downslope toward that tiny village? A village Heart could burn as easily as he had burned the ship?

"Downslope," Jessie shouted. "Now. This way!" Like automatons the sailors turned at her instructions. Why they were running toward the squalid collection of cabins they didn't know, but they were beyond thinking for themselves and they ran on, stumbling, falling, tearing knees, hands, elbows, and faces as they skidded down the hillside.

Above, the Apache rifles opened up, bullets winging around them, ricocheting savagely off stone. The fleeing survivors were into scattered timber now, still running, or trying to, when the long line of men in blue uniforms appeared, riding up the hillside.

"Godfrey," Ki said, laughing out loud. "Remember? Lieutenant Godfrey was coming down to Two Wells to search for Heart. It looks like he's found him."

"It really happens," Jessica Starbuck said before she sagged to the earth to sit there, gulping down deep breaths of air. "The cavalry to the rescue." And then she was laughing, laughing with joy and relief as from the bluff the sounds of battle echoed—Godfrey and his cavalry contingent attacking the fleeing Heart.

"Do you think," Ford Gleason asked, sagging beside her, "that the U.S. Cavalry would ever let you down?" He was grinning as he hugged Jessica and she continued to laugh, kissing him at intervals. Frequent intervals.

Ki stood, hands on hips, watching the battle until he could see no more of it, until it was obvious that Heart was in full retreat. On those bluffs Ki doubted that the cavalry would run the man down, but it was possible, possible that the siege of Yuma would be broken for good and all.

Angelina, her dark hair tangled, her face without its powder, its rouge, smudged and scratched—beautiful— stepped up beside Ki and slipped her arm around his waist.

"Finally?" she asked. "Finally it is over?"

"Finally," Ki replied, "it is over."

There might well have been a welcoming celebration the following day when Godfrey's cavalry patrol, with a number of Apache prisoners and the ragged, rescued band of civilians made their appearance in Yuma, but their arrival went virtually unnoticed.

Half of the town, it seemed, was down at the wharves watching Captain Easley steam upriver with the *President Grant*, its whistle blowing, bells clanging, bringing the supplies Yuma needed to live.

And that, Jessie thought, was as it should be.

JAKE LOGAN

___ 07139-1	SOUTH OF THE BORDER	$2.50
___ 07567-2	SLOCUM'S PRIDE	$2.50
___ 07382-3	SLOCUM AND THE GUN-RUNNERS	$2.50
___ 07494-3	SLOCUM'S WINNING HAND	$2.50
___ 08382-9	SLOCUM IN DEADWOOD	$2.50
___ 07973-2	SLOCUM AND THE AVENGING GUN	$2.50
___ 08087-0	THE SUNSHINE BASIN WAR	$2.50
___ 08279-2	VIGILANTE JUSTICE	$2.50
___ 08189-3	JAILBREAK MOON	$2.50
___ 08392-6	SIX GUN BRIDE	$2.50
___ 08076-5	MESCALERO DAWN	$2.50
___ 08539-6	DENVER GOLD	$2.50
___ 08644-X	SLOCUM AND THE BOZEMAN TRAIL	$2.50
___ 08742-5	SLOCUM AND THE HORSE THIEVES	$2.50
___ 08773-5	SLOCUM AND THE NOOSE OF HELL	$2.50
___ 08791-3	CHEYENNE BLOODBATH	$2.50
___ 09088-4	THE BLACKMAIL EXPRESS	$2.50
___ 09111-2	SLOCUM AND THE SILVER RANCH FIGHT	$2.50
___ 09299-2	SLOCUM AND THE LONG WAGON TRAIN	$2.50

Available at your local bookstore or return this form to:

BERKLEY
THE BERKLEY PUBLISHING GROUP, Dept. B
390 Murray Hill Parkway, East Rutherford, NJ 07073

Please send me the titles checked above. I enclose _____. Include $1.00 for postage and handling if one book is ordered; add 25¢ per book for two or more not to exceed $1.75. CA, IL, NJ, NY, PA, and TN residents please add sales tax. Prices subject to change without notice and may be higher in Canada. Do not send cash.

NAME_____

ADDRESS_____

CITY_____STATE/ZIP_____

(Allow six weeks for delivery.)

162b